VAN HELSING™

A novel by Kevin Ryan
Based on a motion picture screenplay
by Stephen Sommers

POCKET **STAR** BOOKS
New York   London   Toronto   Sydney

An *Original* Publication of POCKET BOOKS

 A Pocket Star Book published by
POCKET BOOKS, a division of Simon & Schuster, Inc.
1230 Avenue of the Americas, New York, NY 10020

This book is a work of fiction. Names, characters, places and incidents are products of the author's imagination or are used fictitiously. Any resemblance to actual events or locales or persons, living or dead, is entirely coincidental.

ISBN: 0-7434-9354-0

First Pocket Books paperback edition May 2004

10   9   8   7   6   5   4   3

POCKET STAR BOOKS and colophon are registered trademarks of Simon & Schuster, Inc.

Manufactured in the United States of America

For information regarding special discounts for bulk purchases, please contact Simon & Schuster Special Sales at 1-800-456-6798 or business@simonandschuster.com.

"The world seems full of good men—even if there *are* monsters in it."

—From *Dracula* by Bram Stoker

Prologue

"VICTOR, I'M SO PROUD OF YOU."

Elizabeth leaned forward and Victor Frankenstein felt her warm lips on his cheek. He had to lean down slightly so that she could reach him. Though not tall himself, Victor stood a head higher than his fiancée. Elizabeth's blue eyes beamed at him. He saw in them her excitement, her admiration, and for the thousandth time he hoped that someday he would be worthy of her devotion.

Victor reached up and felt Elizabeth's shoulder-length blond curls, taking her in. As usual, she was neatly dressed, her curls tamed and close to her head. Elizabeth was always meticulous in her appearance—even more so than Victor himself. She had chosen the brown suit and tie he now wore, and as he looked at her she gently pushed back a stray lock of his hair.

As she smiled at him, Victor found that, once again, he was drawing strength from her. It seemed

1

impossible and not very scientific that her small, slim form could transmit strength to him, but it did. She had waited so long for him. There were the years of medical college, and then his decision to change his focus from surgery to research, which would provide a much less secure future. As a researcher, his fortunes would largely be determined by his ability to win grants and fellowships. His success would depend as much on his talents as a presenter and a salesman as it would on his skill as a physician.

And much of that success would depend on what happened in the next hour.

"Good luck, old man," Henry said, shaking his hand. Then his friend playfully batted him on the shoulder, and Victor felt himself returning Henry's goodwill. It was, he realized, the first time he had smiled that day.

Taller than Victor, Henry—with his good looks, dark hair, and thin, neatly trimmed mustache—had enjoyed plenty of female attention when they had been in school together. Henry had been with him when Victor had met Elizabeth, but to Victor's astonishment—and great happiness—Elizabeth had been completely immune to Henry's charm. She had only been interested in Victor, and they had spent hours talking that first night.

Victor was glad Elizabeth and Henry had come. His heart was still hammering in his chest, but he found himself drawing courage from them, from their simple faith in him.

Despite the fact that he was taking a substantial

risk today, he felt a certainty dawning within his breast. He truly was onto something. His theories were revolutionary, but his results were incontrovertible.

"It's time, Victor. Go shake them up a bit," Henry said.

"Good luck, darling," Elizabeth said, and Victor turned and headed into the auditorium. As a student, he had been in that room a thousand times during his years of medical training at Goldstadf. He had even assisted Professor Waldman in teaching first- and second-year courses.

Now Victor felt sweat on his brow. Today the auditorium was full not of eager students but of physicians and professors of medical science—colleagues looking down at the youngest man ever to apply for the Goldstadf Fellowship, the most prestigious fellowship in Romania, and one of the most esteemed in all of Europe. It also carried a rather large grant and access to the university's considerable resources.

Victor took his place by the podium and was warmly greeted by his mentor, Professor Waldman. The doctor had a thick mop of gray hair and bushy gray eyebrows, their salty color showing his age. Still, Waldman's posture was so ramrod straight that he looked like a first-year military cadet rather than a man just a few years from retirement. Waldman's eyes blazed with a keen intelligence that was legendary at the university. Now those eyes were looking at Victor warmly.

Nodding, Victor took his place by the doctor's side.

"And now, esteemed colleagues, it is my pleasure to introduce Dr. Victor von Frankenstein, who two years ago graduated at the top of his class here at the university," Waldman addressed his audience. "A student of mine since his first year, Victor has distinguished himself both as a surgical resident and as my research assistant. He has also been published in both *The Munich Review of Medicine* and *The Paris Journal of Surgical Science*. Today he has a presentation to make of his own work, and though he has kept the subject of it quite secret, I am certain that it will be of great interest to all of us."

His teacher turned to him and whispered, "They are all yours, Victor."

Victor nodded and took the podium as the professor stepped away. Quickly scanning the audience, Victor relaxed a bit as he spied Elizabeth and Henry taking their seats in an upper row of the auditorium. Once again he took strength from them, then began: "Distinguished guests, I welcome you." As he spoke, Victor felt his confidence grow. His work was important and he would do it justice today.

"I am pleased to see so many well-known faces from all of the fields of medical science. Surgery, orthopedics, internal medicine, and neurology. With all due modesty, I can assure you that what I am about to propose will be of interest to each and every one of you, and will have dramatic implications in all of our various fields of study.

"Nearly two thousand five hundred years ago,

Hippocrates changed the field of medicine forever by establishing once and for all that there were no supernatural causes for disease, only natural ones. A few hundred years later, Galen developed the first medical theories based on the principles of scientific experimentation. In the centuries since that time, we have used experiments to learn more and more about those natural causes. Recently, Louis Pasteur revealed a microscopic world of germs. We continue to learn about anatomy and of the body as a machine. Today, our treatments and surgical techniques improve at a rate that would astonish Hippocrates, and we have learned more in the last century than we had in the nearly two millennia that came before. At the threshold of the twentieth century, we stand on the brink of new and exciting discoveries.

"However, significant mysteries still remain. All of us have seen cases that defy our explanation. We have seen identical patients with identical illnesses, some who survive, some who do not. Why does pneumonia sometimes take a healthy young man from us and at other times allow an elderly man to recover? What are the forces that promote healing? Hasten death? Why do some patients mend more quickly than others, while some never at all?"

"God," someone remarked a bit too loudly, which elicited a low laughter from the audience.

Victor smiled. He was ready for this. "Yes, perhaps God has a plan for each of us that predetermines how long we live and when we die. Yet, has God not also allowed our medical science to intervene and save lives? If this is so, then healers are truly doing His work."

The laughter ceased and Victor paused for a moment to consider his colleagues. He sensed they were prepared for what would come next. "I submit to you that there is a force underlying all of our work . . . a force hitherto invisible . . . a force of life." The audience was quite attentive now, many in it straining forward.

"We have known for some time about the role of electricity in the human body. The fields of chemical galvanism and electro-biology were born more than a hundred years ago, when Luigi Galvani caused the leg of a recently deceased frog to twitch through the application of electricity. My subsequent work has suggested the existence of a force underlying even electrical impulses: a life force, if you will. I submit to you that this life force can be manipulated and focused through the careful application of electrical and magnetic forces— that this life force can actually be harnessed to promote health and healing."

Immediately the room broke out into dozens of separate conversations. Victor heard shock and indignation in the murmuring voices.

"Gentlemen, please!" Professor Waldman's voice boomed, silencing some but not all of the discussion.

"I know that what I am proposing is revolutionary," Victor continued. "However, is it really any more revolutionary than Pasteur's work? He introduced us to an invisible world of microscopic organisms. Is it so hard to believe that there is even more we do not know, even more that we do not see?"

"What are you suggesting? That there is a magic ray that will heal a broken limb, close a wound, clear a body of disease?" shouted a voice from the audience.

"No more magic than sulfur powder," Victor countered.

"And what if you applied enough of this 'life force' to Galvani's dead frog? Are you saying it could get up and hop away?" hooted another.

Victor answered without hesitation, "Theoretically, yes, but—"

The response was immediate. Half of the room erupted into cries of scorn, the other half into peals of laughter. Victor felt his cheeks flush, even as his own internal temperature seemed to go up ten degrees.

"Blasphemy!" a voice yelled out.

Victor found himself roaring back, "No, not blasphemy! *Science!*" All conversation ceased for a moment before degenerating again into chaos.

Professor Waldman called out and in a few minutes order was restored.

When the auditorium was quiet once more, Victor said, "I know that what I am proposing is extraordinary, but I ask you to read the contents of the folder now in front of each of you. It contains all of my experimental records and the findings of my research."

Looking out over the crowd, Victor saw nothing

7

but blank faces. The response to his fellowship application would not come for weeks; however, he already knew what that reply would be.

Victor knew that he had failed: He had failed his work . . . he had failed himself, and . . . and, worst of all, he had failed Elizabeth. Still, he held his head up high, met the crowd's eyes one last time, and said, "I thank you for your time."

His face burning, Victor walked off. Even as he left the auditorium, he heard the disapproving voices of his colleagues. For this distinguished group, it was the equivalent of catcalls and the hurling of fruit and vegetables.

He stood alone in the hallway for a brief moment and then saw Professor Waldman approach him. "Victor, are you all right?"

"Fine, Professor . . . but it would appear that my career is over."

Waldman shook his head. "You always have a place with me. There is a great deal we can do together."

Victor knew this already. Waldman's research was good science. And the professor was making slow and steady progress: new procedures, new techniques. But Victor could not shake the feeling that a position with Waldman was all a waste of time, compared to what he *could* be doing, to what he *could* be accomplishing. He knew that in a decade his pioneering work on the life force could do more to advance medicine than the last two thousand years of study by the best minds in the world. Within just a few years, he could dwarf what Waldman had done in his entire career.

Perhaps it *was* arrogant and prideful of him to think it. But it was also true.

"No, thank you, Professor," Victor said simply.

Waldman studied him for a minute. "Please, Victor. This was merely a setback. Do not let it consume you, and please promise me that you will at least consider my offer."

Victor could only nod, and the professor turned away as Henry and Elizabeth approached.

It was a full four weeks before Victor returned to his family home in Romania. He had promised Elizabeth a holiday and he had made good on his word. However, his mind had never really been on the trip and she had known it. Even in their beautiful rented villa on the Seine, he had been unable to relax. Part of the problem was that he did not feel he was being fair to Elizabeth, given his new professional circumstances.

After a few days Victor had sat down to talk seriously with his fiancée. "Elizabeth, I want . . . I need to continue my work, on my own if I have to. There are the family holdings, a little income. I can set up a lab in the house. It won't have the staff or advantages of the university, but it's a start." His family had some means, although their fortunes were not what they once were.

"I understand," Elizabeth had responded.

"I'm not sure you do, darling. It will be some time

before my work will bring results." Science, even revolutionary science, depended on experiments, data, and reproducible results. There would be years of working with animals and lower life-forms, and he would have to make do with the equipment he could afford.

"The point is, Elizabeth, it'll be some time before I will have achieved anything substantial. For some time I will be the laughingstock that I was at Gold-stadf." He didn't know how to put into words what he knew had to come next. As it turned out, Elizabeth wasn't going to let him.

"None of that matters to me, Victor. I know what you are. You are the man I love. And I know I have to share you with your work," she said before he could interrupt. "If you think that I will allow this little setback to delay our life together, you are very mistaken, Dr. Victor Frankenstein. I mean to marry you and I do not mean to wait."

"But, Elizabeth, I can't offer you—"

"You have offered me yourself and that is all I want. I won't be stopped by money or the Goldstadf Fellowship board or anything else. And I can assist you in your work."

"We wouldn't have much to start," Victor had said.

"We will have everything we need," Elizabeth had replied.

At that moment, Victor had felt the cloud that had descended on him during his disastrous presentation lift. There was hope—not only for his work, but for his life with Elizabeth.

It might not be the Goldstadf Fellowship, but it was enough for him.

Now he walked into the family home with his few servants standing ready to greet him. It was good to be back. It was evening before he had his belongings unpacked and attended to his responsibilities as master of the house.

There was quite a large pile of correspondence demanding his attention, but Victor decided to forgo that until the morrow. He sat at his desk and began making notes: If he was going to outfit a lab in his own home, he would have much to do.

He smiled as he imagined Elizabeth sitting down at the same moment to make plans for the wedding. Yes, together they could accomplish quite a bit.

Less than an hour into his work, Victor's butler, Gerald, came to inform him that there was someone at the door. Before he spoke, Gerald cleared his throat dramatically. "A Count Dracula. I asked him to return in the morning, but he was quite insistent that he see you. I'm sorry, sir, the hour is quite indecent."

It was unusual. He had heard of *a* Count Dracula, but this could not be *that* Dracula. Poor Gerald looked distressed. "It's quite all right. Let's go see to our guest."

The foyer was empty, and Victor flashed Gerald a look.

"He would not leave, but he would not enter," Gerald said.

His natural curiosity piqued, Victor went to the

front door and came face-to-face with a tall man standing in the entryway. He was dressed all in black, a long coat draping his body. The clothing was formal and had a vaguely military look, of a style Victor had never seen before. Most unusual was his hair, which was long, dark, and pulled back, away from his face. Perhaps the oddest thing about him was the single earring he wore in his left ear—a small golden hoop. Clearly the count was nobility, but Victor had never known an aristocrat who wore an *earring*.

The count's features were striking, with pronounced cheekbones and very dark hair. If Victor had had to guess, he would have said the man was perhaps thirty, just a little older than Victor himself. His guest certainly looked like a man in the prime of youth, but there was something odd about his eyes, which looked older than his face—much older. Victor found himself drawn to those eyes. They were electric, intense, and . . . warm? No, just very *interested* in him. After a few moments, Victor realized that he had been staring. He shook his head; he was being rude.

"Count Dracula, I presume," he said, offering his hand.

The man nodded curtly and said, "Yes, Dr. Frankenstein. It is a true pleasure to meet you."

"Why are you waiting outside?" Victor asked.

"I would not presume to enter without an invitation from the master of the house. Particularly at this *indecent hour*," Dracula said, giving Gerald a quick look. Victor had the feeling that Count Dracula had somehow overheard their conversation, but of course that was impossible. Gerald seemed unnerved by the count's attention. His butler had been with the family since Victor was a boy, and he had never seen the man as uncomfortable as now.

"By all means, do come in," Victor said.

Dracula stepped over the threshold and Victor felt a sudden chill, quickly dismissing it as the result of a cool evening breeze. "Brandy?" he offered.

"Yes, thank you."

"Gerald, we will take it in the library." Victor led the count to the comfortable chairs in front of the fire, where they were surrounded by his family's many books.

"My arrival is clearly a surprise to you. I apologize for that and for the lateness of the hour."

Victor tried but failed to place the count's accent. The Romanian was fluent, but he spoke it with a trace of something else. . . . "Quite all right," he said.

"I wrote you some time ago announcing my impending visit," the count continued.

"I have been traveling, and I must have not opened your letter yet," Victor replied. Then Gerald arrived with the brandy.

Victor raised his glass to his guest. "Cheers."

The count returned the gesture, but put the glass down without drinking.

"I don't mean to be rude, but perhaps later," Dracula said.

Victor noted that it was odd behavior, but no less than having an aristocrat show up at one's door after ten in the evening. "What can I do for you, Count Dracula?"

The count smiled, but the gesture was joyless and never reached his eyes—eyes that were now boring into Victor, so much so that he found it almost frightening. The feeling passed and Victor realized that he was being silly. The count had been nothing but courteous and was his guest, after all.

"I am very interested in your work. I have learned of your presentation to the university and managed to obtain a copy of your Goldstadf Fellowship application materials. I found your theories quite thought-provoking indeed."

Victor stared blankly at his guest for a hint of irony or mockery. He detected none, seeing nothing but sincerity. Until now, the only people inquiring about Victor's work were journalists who wanted to ridicule him.

"I am quite serious, I assure you," the count went on, perhaps reading his thoughts. "I have from time to time been a benefactor of scientific research. I am here to speak with you about a grant. I think your work could be very important. I have significant means and have begun to think about my legacy on this world."

His eyes looked at Victor with an intensity that made him both nervous and giddy with excitement.

"Surely, as a physician, you have imagined the enormous potential impact of your theory on the force of life. If it could indeed be harnessed, the results for mankind could be revolutionary."

Victor could not hide his surprise, or his pleasure. "I have seen great potential in my work, but so far I have been alone in my enthusiasm."

"Then allow me to offer my support . . . and my friendship. Perhaps together we can realize that potential. Then you can take your place among Hippocrates, Pasteur, and the giants of medicine."

Those eyes. They were magnetic, drawing Victor in and making him believe the offer of brotherhood and support—of the kind that he had not had from a single human being. The count was his only friend.

No, that's not true, Victor thought. *Elizabeth is that and more. And what of Henry?* He had only just met Dracula. The bright sincerity in Elizabeth's eyes came to Victor's mind, but he found that he was uncomfortable thinking of her in his visitor's presence.

Victor had the brief, uncanny feeling that Dracula had opened a window into his mind. "I was thinking of equipping you with a full laboratory. New equipment. Anything you require to speed your research."

"My good count, I'm afraid that that is a large order. The cost would be considerable. Much of the equipment would have to be designed and built to new specifications. That is why I approached the university: I hoped to involve the physical sciences and chemistry departments.

"I assure you that my means *are* considerable. Whatever you need, you shall have. Just think of what we can accomplish together!"

The count rose to leave. "Begin making a list of what you require," he said. "If it is acceptable to you,

I shall return tomorrow evening and we shall discuss the matter further."

Victor walked his guest to the door and bade him good night. "I don't know how to thank you, Count Dracula."

The count simply nodded and shook Victor's hand. Victor thought it felt unusually cold. Then Dracula broke the contact, looked him once more in the eye, and turned to leave.

Seconds later, Count Dracula disappeared into the night.

With his strange visitor's departure, Frankenstein felt dizzy, as if he had stood up too quickly. Had he just dreamed the whole encounter?

"Master Frankenstein? Has your guest left?" Gerald asked from beside him.

"Yes. That will be all for the night, Gerald. Thank you."

"Very well, sir," Gerald replied, and headed back down the hallway.

So it wasn't a dream. So much the better, Victor thought. Certainly the count was the answer to his prayers.

I'm lucky to have a friend like him.

No. He had just met Count Dracula. They were just acquaintances, not friends. *Not yet.*

Far too excited to sleep tonight, Victor went back to his office and set to work.

He would have to cancel his plans with Elizabeth for tomorrow so he could labor through the day as well. The count was offering him the opportunity of a lifetime; to be ready for their next meeting was the least he could do.

Victor felt a rush of hope for the future. *Soon, the whole world will know the name* Frankenstein.

Something was nagging at him through the reverie, though—something odd. And he soon realized what it was.

Dracula had arrived at his door in the dead of night, but there had been no coach waiting for him. Not even a horse in the drive.

1

DR. FRANKENSTEIN MADE HIS FINAL ADJUSTMENT.

"Igor, check the conductors."

His assistant made a face and turned to walk up the stairs. His defining feature was his twisted back, which forced him to hunch sharply to one side, making his gait unsteady. His features were blunt and, oddly, he had no eyebrows over his small, deep-set, and perpetually red-rimmed eyes. Long, stringy red hair hung down past the man's face, only adding to his peculiar looks.

Frankenstein had had doubts about hiring Igor to assist him in the lab. It was not his appearance, though he knew most others were put off by Igor's misshapen form, and Gerald and the other servants voiced concerns about him as well. Frankenstein understood their worry, but his friend Count Dracula had felt strongly about Igor. Besides, as a scientist, he preferred to deal with the real, the tangible—with things that could be quantified.

And as a physician, Frankenstein understood the nature and cause of the deformity and had at one time dedicated his life to healing people such as Igor. In a rush of excitement, he realized that he was about to succeed beyond his wildest dreams. Even Gerald would be impressed, and he had rarely seen his servant excited about anything.

But Gerald is gone. . . .

Yes . . . all of them were gone. Gerald had stayed the longest, his loyalty to the family running the deepest. Still, they had all left one by one. That had been what? A year ago? No, closer to two.

On a certain level, Frankenstein understood why. He had changed. His Work had completely absorbed him, and had let many other things slip. Even now he could not remember the last time he had rested. Sleep was not the pleasure it once was: dark dreams always came to him. His only release was his Work, where he could be lost and forget about everything else . . .

. . . even Elizabeth.

It hurt to think of her, so much so that the count had urged him many times not to. Dracula wanted what was best for him, for his Work. The count was helping him take his place with Hippocrates, Pasteur . . . the giants of medicine.

Great deeds required great sacrifice—sacrifices like Elizabeth.

No! part of his mind rebelled. *I do not want to give her up. . . .*

But he had. She stayed longer than the others, but then she, too, had abandoned him. It had been inevitable; she had never liked the count and was interfering with his Work—the Work that was almost finished.

When he had succeeded, he would win Elizabeth back. They would all come back. . . .

Yet, part of him knew it was too late. Too much had happened. Looking around his lab, he wondered what his father would think of what he had done to the watchtower of Castle Frankenstein. Then he was jolted by the realization that this was not his ancestral home. The count had Frankenstein move his lab to the Transylvanian region of Romania, and had provided him with this castle. It was a very generous gift: Dracula was truly his friend.

It was here that Frankenstein had installed the dynamos, the generators, the powerful electromagnets, the chemical-reaction tanks. They represented the best German engineering, much of it based on Frankenstein's own designs and all of it made possible by his friend the count. As he looked around, he saw progress, the future. There were machines—creations of man—about to aid him in the ultimate act of creation. If he were still alive, his father would appreciate that much, even if he might not understand all the science.

There was something else here, though, something that his father would not have approved of. It wasn't the dust, grime, and cobwebs that covered much of the lab. It wasn't even in the rank smells, the leftovers of previous, failed experiments. It was the overwhelming stench of corruption.

More sacrifices for his Work, which had gone much faster than expected. The count had pushed Frankenstein to be more *aggressive*. The experiments on humans began almost immediately. There had been the ethical questions, of course, but Dracula had allayed all of his concerns.

And the count was his friend.

There had been some intoxicating victories. If only he could have published the results, then the fools on the Goldstadf Fellowship review board would know how wrong they had been in scorning him. They would see the genius of Frankenstein. Yes, *genius*. He would not deny the simple truth now, any more than he would rob himself of the triumph that he knew was within his grasp.

"The conductors are secure, Doctor," Igor called from the stairs.

Frankenstein raced across the room and checked his generators. Gauges showed that they were operating at full power. He flipped the first switch, the hum of the equipment rising in pitch. Then he activated more switches, careful to maintain the correct sequence as he turned on the electromagnets and dynamos and finally engaged the chemical-reaction tanks.

Electricity arced across contact points, and the hum increased in volume. The sound was intoxicating. It was the call of new life waiting to be born. Frankenstein spent minutes more adjusting, calibrating. The convergence of forces had to be just right. Electricity and magnetism along with chemical catalysts had to be perfectly aligned to bring about the primal energies he sought to summon.

When he was satisfied that all was in order, he moved to the structure that dominated the center of the room—a very special pod that looked like an oversize surgical table connected to electrodes and his precious equipment. On it lay his greatest creation: the Work incarnate.

A large figure covered in bandages, sewn together by Frankenstein's own hands. Pieces from cadavers carefully selected and assembled using surgical techniques that his colleagues had yet to imagine. Yet, it was only the beginning.

Even now, life was beginning to flow into his creation. Nerves, bone, and sinew were healing on the cellular level. It was not yet alive, but it was no longer completely dead.

Frankenstein knew he had nothing to do now but wait. Looking down at its closed eyes, he whispered, "You are truly my son."

The only one I will ever know, a voice in his mind supplied.

This new truth awakened in him feelings he had never known. With Elizabeth gone, there would be no children . . . no family . . . not with her—and if so, then not with anyone.

"You are my legacy to the world and I shall love you like my own son," Frankenstein said. Tears ran freely down his face. He could not tell if they were for his old life or for the new one before him. In the end it didn't matter; he simply let them come.

"And I shall do right by you," he promised. In his visible form, his son was not aesthetically pleasing. He wished he had done better, more careful work in the assembly. But the count had been in such a hurry.

And the count is my . . .

Frankenstein found that he did not want to think of Dracula now. This moment was for father and son alone. Once he was alive, his son's form would be perfected; he would be the first to receive the benefits of Frankenstein's work.

Lightning flashed in the distance. Frankenstein counted off two seconds before the crack of thunder came. Two miles away. Closer than the last one.

"I give you life. And I shall see that life nurtured. I have failed many, but I shall not fail you. With your life, I give you the will to live it. The free will that is the right of all men," Frankenstein declared.

Another flash, another thunderclap. This one was less than a mile away. It wouldn't be long now. There were other sounds coming from outside, voices, shouting. Frankenstein knew he should be concerned but could not take his attention away from his task for an instant. After coming this far, he merely willed the lightning to approach.

All the while, his machinery worked, delivering its power to his son. He felt the connection between them growing. It was something he had not counted on—a finding he had not anticipated. Still, he welcomed it.

More dazzling light; the thunder was very near.

His equipment was crucial, but the final breath of life and the incredible energies that it would require would come from above . . .

. . . from the heavens.

Suddenly, Frankenstein knew that he was only part of a plan—one that was not his. For an instant he had fancied himself as a master of creation. But he was not the master here. No matter. He had his son now and he would make everything right.

It came.

Frankenstein saw the lightning strike before it actually hit the conductors on the roof of the watchtower. He felt it when the force that would fulfill his vision touched the machines. They sprang to life first, gathering the incredible power of the universe into the crystal diffuser Frankenstein had placed into his son's chest. Electricity arced across the length of the laboratory, and life surged into his son. Then, as quickly as it had come, the flash of energy disappeared and his son's eyes flickered.

The scream came from a deeper place in himself than Frankenstein knew existed. "He's alive. . . . He's alive. . . . HE'S ALIIIIVE!!!"

The euphoria was indescribable, maybe what God Himself must have known in His greatest moment of creation. Now all of his sacrifices seemed worth it, as he had achieved something that no one else in the history of mankind had even attempted.

A loud crash brought him out of his bliss. There was the sound of splintering wood, angry voices. Running to a window, he saw a torch-carrying mob outside in the night. He recognized one of them: a tall man wearing a large top hat. Frankenstein knew why they had come, and felt a chill as he realized that their anger was righteous. If he could only talk to them, he would explain why some of his *unconventional* methods had been necessary.

Some were carrying a tree trunk. They surged forward, charging the castle's front gate. Another crash. Wood splintered, but the gate held, though Frankenstein knew it would not be for long.

Screaming, more fury from below. He would have no time to justify his work and its incredible value. His creation—his son—was in danger. They would never understand. The mob would look upon his son and see only a monster. Where was his friend, the count? Dracula should be helping him, protecting him, so why was he abandoning him now?

"Success!" a voice cried out from behind him.

Frankenstein spun around and found himself face-to-face with a dark figure. The fear in his stomach reached his throat and he screamed. Then he recognized the familiar features and felt the terror briefly subside.

"Oh . . . Count . . . it's just you," Frankenstein said, glad to see his last remaining friend.

Dracula stepped forward into the flickering lights created by the surging electricity all around them. There was something wrong. His voice was flat, toneless, and his eyes were like ice.

"I was beginning to lose faith, Victor." Then the count looked down at the villagers. "A pity your moment of triumph is being spoiled over a little thing like grave robbery."

The mob surged forward, the villagers moving through the night as if they were a single living organism with just one purpose: revenge. They still could not comprehend why anyone—let alone someone who called himself a doctor—could commit such unspeakable and unholy acts as grave robbery. But whatever the motive, the desecrations had driven their entire town into a frenzied state of horror and outrage. Though not all or even most of them had been wronged, they would have vengeance just the same.

Most carried torches and all carried weapons, makeshift arms of pitchforks, shovels, and axes—tools for tilling and tending the land that would be put to a much darker purpose this night.

They prepared for another run at the gate with their tree-trunk battering ram as the new Castle Frankenstein rose out of the moors in front of them.

Centuries old, the castle had withstood invading armies, but the villagers were certain that it would fall to them tonight. There would only be one man inside, and they would have him before the evening was through.

At the head of the organism was the village undertaker in his top hat. His eyes reflected the torch he wielded and a gleam that showed genuine pleasure at the task at hand. He urged them on with cries of encouragement. "You know what he's doing in there—to the bodies of your loved ones!"

A roar rose up around him. The men holding the tree trunk went at it again. The weakening gate still held, as if reluctant to give up the fight.

Again, Frankenstein was struck by the lack of concern in the count's voice. Grave robbery was a serious charge. The mob would be through the castle gate soon. From there, the front door would be little trouble . . . then there would be no stopping them.

Frankenstein looked pleadingly at Dracula and said, "I must . . . I must escape from this place."

With growing panic, Frankenstein raced through his laboratory, seeing it as if for the first time. It looked more like a rank dungeon than a place of scholarly scientific research. The machinery and equipment that had once thrilled him were now frightening. The dynamos, the generators, the chemical vats, and reaction chambers were grotesque, abominations churning away as his world crumbled around him.

Something was terribly wrong here. The count was viewing him with something like contempt, only much worse—surely not friendship. In the blink of an eye, the one certainty in his life vanished and threatened to take the rest of his mind with it.

The count's voice materialized from above: "Where are you going to run, Victor?"

Dracula was now impossibly high up in the rafters, as if he had been magically transported there. If it was magic, then it was a very dark art, indeed, Frankenstein realized.

It was too much to take in all at once, so he tried to focus. Throwing open a nearby traveling chest, Frankenstein wildly began packing. He had to get away, to get his creation away from here . . . away from the mob . . . away from Dracula. Then he would sort out what was happening.

"Your peculiar experiments have made you . . . *unwelcome* in most of the civilized world." Dracula's voice was cold with just a hint of mockery. Frankenstein looked up and saw that the count was now somehow on the other side of the room, pacing on the great mantelpiece over the fire.

It didn't make sense. It defied the laws of physics and motion as he understood them. Who was this man, really? He had lied to Frankenstein—from the beginning. And the count had taken something important from him.

No, I gave it to him. I invited him into my home. And I have invited him into more than that.

Frankenstein forced himself to concentrate on the only thing that mattered now: his son. "I'll take him away, far away, where no one will ever find him." He continued packing, just the things he would need, but it was so hard to think with the count nearby.

Suddenly, Dracula was right next to him, stepping down on the lid of the trunk and slamming it shut. "No, Victor. The time has come for *me* to take command of him."

"What are you saying?" Frankenstein's voice sounded nearly hysterical to his own ears.

"Why do you think I brought you here? Gave you this castle? Equipped your lab?"

The scientist in him struggled to understand, even as he feared the harrowing implications. "You said you believed in my work. . . ." *That I would take my place among the giants. . . .*

"And I do. But now that it is, as you yourself said, 'a triumph of science over God,' it must serve *my* purpose."

"What purpose?" Frankenstein looked for answers in the count's icy gaze. He felt the last remnants of Dracula's hold on him disappear—not because Frankenstein had broken free, but because the count had released him . . . because Frankenstein had fulfilled the man's evil purpose. He was certain now of one thing: His creation—his son—was to be taken from him.

As one, the villagers raced forward again, the makeshift battering ram slamming into the castle gate, unyielding metal now twisting and groaning. Cheers of excitement rose, and though they were near exhaustion, the men holding the tree trunk quickly took position for another run.

The gate was no match for their irresistible force—seconds later they were finally through. Victorious cries rippled through the crowd as they made their way toward their quarry. The man in the top hat looked on and urged them to continue, grinning wickedly from ear to ear.

* * *

Frankenstein understood what he had allowed to enter his life, and what he might set loose on the world. Nothing that he thought or felt could be measured, quantified and reduced to experimental results. But he was sure it was all as real as the life he had created—the very life that Dracula would use against mankind.

"Good Lord . . . ," Frankenstein said, evoking God for the first time in longer than he could remember. He would not be part of these fiendish designs any longer. "I would kill myself before helping in such a task."

"Feel free. I don't actually need *you* anymore, Victor. I just need *him*," the count said pointing to the table. *"He* is the key."

Dracula stepped toward him and Frankenstein could feel the pure malice radiating from the . . . *creature*. For whatever the count was, he was certainly not a man.

Victor backed away, toward the fireplace. He set his jaw and narrowed his eyes. To his surprise, he felt defiant, even in the face of inhuman strength and dark power. He knew his body was weak: He had slept little in the last few months and could not even remember his last meal. However, he had to protect his creation and do something to put a stop to this madness.

"Before I would allow him to be used for such evil, I would destroy him."

"I can't allow that to happen. My brides would be very put out."

"Igor! Help me!" Frankenstein called out. He would fight this creature to his dying breath, but he also knew he would likely lose.

"You have been so kind to me, Doctor, so caring and thoughtful," Igor said from a safe distance. "But if they catch me, they'll hang me again." The assistant gave him a joyless smile and revealed his horribly disfigured and broken neck. No one would rescue Victor from the hellspawn Dracula, or the crowd that might even now be seconds away.

But he still had himself, and the count would have to reckon with the last of the Frankensteins. Moving quickly, Victor reached above the mantel and pulled a saber that was crossed over the family coat of arms. The weight of his family's ancient weapon felt good in his hands. He felt righteous anger, the power of his father and all of his ancestors, arming him, strengthening him, and steadying his hand.

"Stay back," he commanded.

His adversary stepped toward him. "You can't kill me, Victor . . . ," Dracula said. Then, unbelievably, the count *stepped into Frankenstein's saber*, its blade piercing his chest. For a moment Victor was too shocked to move. He could only watch in horror as the count kept walking, impaling himself further and finally bringing himself to within inches of his face.

"I'm *already* dead," Dracula whispered.

Thought was momentarily impossible. Victor struggled to understand what had just occurred as he faced this . . . *abomination* of nature—one who, it seemed, had long ago discovered his own means of immortality that now flew in the face of mere science.

My God, what have I done?

You knew what you were doing, the long-lost voice of reason murmured inside his head. *All along, you knew this was too good to be true. Everyone tried to warn you about the count . . . what he was really capable of . . . but you ignored them . . . you turned them away one by one in the name of the Work . . . always the Work.*

My son . . . forgive me.

He watched as Dracula's canine teeth seemed to grow in front of him, becoming razor-sharp fangs. All color drained from the monster's once-human face. As Victor looked into those cold, dead eyes, he felt all of his defiance and hope leave him. He had been the architect of his own destruction, but he did not regret his own imminent death; he had brought it on himself.

His only regret was that his creation would now fall under the power of this monster. *His son* deserved better.

Dracula leaned down and Victor knew he had seconds to live. Staring into that monster's face was like looking into the face of Satan himself . . . or as close to the Devil as he would ever see in this world and perhaps even the next.

Victor felt a pressure on his neck as those long teeth pierced his skin, somehow reaching much farther than could be measured. The physician inside

33

him knew that Dracula was drawing his blood, but another part of him knew that the count was taking much more than that.

Darkness loomed, enveloped him, and he knew no more.

Noise. Light. Difficult to focus. He did not know where he was and could not remember his name. But someone was nearby.

Father.

Yes, Father had spoken to him while he . . . slept? It was hard to remember. His thoughts were scattered and he had to focus them. Even as he tried, sleep beckoned and something even deeper called to him. He fought it.

He was strong. That was his second certainty. *Father had made him strong.* He forced his eyes to stay open. Soon they adjusted to the bright light. There were flashes everywhere, but he could make out shapes if he tried very hard.

He realized that he was looking at the place of Father's Work, where he was given shape and then life. He heard Father's voice, he recognized it as the voice in his dream. He wanted to see him, to touch him. To hear that voice clearly, the voice that had called him into the world.

But something was pressing down on him. He was on a table. *Pod* came into his mind: It was Father's word for the thing that held him now. He pushed against it. Why hadn't Father come to release him?

There were two voices. One was Father's and there was another that he did not recognize. Father sounded upset . . . and *frightened*. He could hear it in his voice, and also *feel* it somewhere deeper inside him.

The straps that held him would not move. He strained against them. Father needed him and he pushed harder.

Something broke and one of his bonds was off him. He snapped the others easily, then hesitated. There was danger here, and he would have to be careful. He moved slowly, which was all he could manage. His limbs were powerful, but he had to concentrate to control their movements.

He looked for Father and found him pointing a weapon at the Other Man. The stranger was approaching Father, wanting to hurt him. There was not much time and they were too far away. He watched as the Other Man leaned down and *bit* Father.

He felt Father's pain and knew that he would not reach them in time. He was not quick enough.

But he was strong.

He reached down and took hold of one of the machines. It was large, and very heavy, but that did not matter. He lifted it easily off the ground. With Father in danger, the weight was nothing to him.

Then he saw the Other Man drop Father to the floor and he felt a change in himself, as if that which had been connecting him to Father had suddenly been severed. A loud sound escaped from his throat, and with a single heave, he threw the machine at the Other Man.

It sailed through the air and hit him squarely, knocking him off his feet and carrying him into the fireplace. Moving as quickly as he could, he approached Father, taking his Creator into his arms.

He saw movement ahead of him. It was not the Other Man, but someone Father knew. Igor, he was called. The little man was leaving—fleeing. He followed from a safe distance. Carrying Father, he moved down the stairs, gaining more strength and better control over his own movements, his mind growing clearer by the second.

Igor disappeared into a doorway. He pursued and found himself in a small, dark hall. Then he saw another door at the end. He went to it, pushed the door open, and found himself outside.

Igor was in his way, so he shoved hard and headed across the field. Behind him, he heard a voice shout, "Frankenstein! He's created a monster!"

He immediately realized two things: Frankenstein was Father's name, and that the "monster" was *him*. He heard the angry mob and knew that he and Father were still in danger. He forged on without looking back, heading for a building in the distance.

He and Father could rest there; but even as he thought it, he worried that Father might be beyond all hope. The Other Man had done something terrible to him.

A fading voice cried out, "Look! It's headed for the windmill!"

He weighed the danger of continuing. If the angry people followed him . . .

Father is beyond hurting now, a voice inside him said.

No. Father was a great man, and without Father he had nothing. He had to get to safety, to help the man to whom he owed everything.

He ran.

Minutes later he was at the door to the building. It was chained and secured, but with one hand he pulled the door open. He heard the people outside, then saw them with their torches. He slammed the door shut behind him. Inside, there was a machine and a smell he recognized: alcohol. There were stairs. He climbed them quickly. Father needed him.

For a moment, Dracula was too stunned to move. He felt the weight of the machine on him and he allowed the heat to burn his skin. He had been surprised; that creature had surprised *him.* That had not happened in decades, perhaps longer.

Dracula had assumed it would be no more than a mindless beast, even if Frankenstein had succeeded in his work. But that thing had actually *cared* for the blithering fool who had created it.

And Frankenstein *had* been a fool—brilliant, perhaps a genius, even, but that mind had been pathetically easy to gain entrance into. The most intelligent of the living thought that they were somehow impervious to manipulation. But their very vanity and pride opened many doors to him.

In his centuries, Dracula had known many such minds. He had known stronger ones, too, but in the end they had either fallen to him or perished.

He would not be thwarted for an instant by Frankenstein's creature. Of course, it would die, but not before serving Dracula's purpose and his will.

The count looked forward to destroying the creature when the time came. He pushed the machine off himself and charged out of the fireplace. Though his face was burned, it took but a minute to change that; his ability to regenerate at will was another example of how far superior he was to the living.

Another moment of concentration and Dracula summoned his winged form. He took a second to relish the power of this incarnation and the fear his appearance struck in mortals. They had a preternatural fear of bats—one that was in this case very well founded.

As Dracula took flight, he saw his shadow falling over the laboratory walls—soon it would cover much more. Frankenstein's creature was the key, and Dracula meant to have him.

Frankenstein's creation reached the top. Outside again, he could see the castle in the distance. The line of incensed, shouting people quickly surrounded the windmill.

Nothing happened for a few seconds, and he hoped that they would leave him and Father in peace. He had not harmed anyone. The night was still and the crowd suddenly fell silent. Torchlight illuminated their prey, and as one, they caught their first look at the ghastly construct that loomed above them.

Then someone stepped forward and flung a torch,

breaking both the silence and the stillness. The outcry resumed, and more torches flew toward the very old wooden structure.

Danger! his mind screamed. He and Father could not stay where they were. And they could not go down.

He struggled to understand their fear, their hatred, their desire to do him harm. "Why . . . ?" he asked of them.

As the flames grew higher, the people below became quiet again, satisfied that he and Father would soon be destroyed. The new silence was broken, this time by the shattering of glass. A dark shape emerged from the top of the castle. Though still too far to see clearly, he knew it was the Other Man. He looked like a winged shadow and was soon joined by three others. There was something wrong with their liquid movement through the night sky—something that was unnatural.

"Vampires!" someone in the crowd shrieked. "Run for your lives!"

So even the mob knew that the Other Man was dangerous. But Father had trusted him once. And then . . .

He looked down and saw his creator, still and wan in the light of the flames that now licked around him. He pulled the great man to his chest and held him tightly but gently in his arms.

"Father . . . ," he said.

He felt tears run down his face as he realized that Father truly was gone. Even if the fire and the vampires disappeared, Father would be no more. Fury rose in his chest as he saw the liquid shadows coming closer. Holding Father with one hand, he lifted the other to the sky. The angry people, the vampires . . . they wanted to hurt those who had done them no harm.

He gave his anger voice, bellowing out his rage and pain. He felt the heat of the flames and knew there was no way out. A loud roar suddenly rose from the depths of the old building, and the world seemed to come apart around him.

He had just an instant to realize that his end had come. There was fire and great weight on his body as the windmill disintegrated. Still clutching Father, he fell and blackness consumed him.

Dracula witnessed the windmill implode, crashing to the ground in burning ruins. *"No!"* he screamed as he swooped down, taking his customary form as he came to earth. Running, he approached the wreckage.

Gone. There could be nothing left alive in there. The living were pitifully weak, their bodies easily succumbing to injury and illness. He sensed his brides near him: Aleera, Verona, and Marishka. He did not have to see their faces to read the horror.

Stumbling closer to the destruction, he heard his women wailing and shrieking. To the sounds of their cries, the fire threw up its last sparks . . . then went out as their hopes for the future died with it.

That creature . . . , he cursed inwardly. It was the second time Dracula had been surprised by Franken-stein's monster. A pity the thing was already dead— the count would have relished killing him.

2

Vatican City, Rome
One Year Later

A MAN DRESSED COMPLETELY IN BLACK APPROACHED THE gates of the Vatican. He was tall, with a large cloak that billowed after him in the early morning light. A wide-brimmed hat partly covered his face, and one had to come fairly close to see his long hair and countenance, which was handsome but unshaven and careworn. The man's eyes were dark and his mouth set, perhaps even cruel, though no one ventured near enough to see these details.

As he entered the gates, the guards watched him carefully. The Vatican was the seat of the Roman Catholic Church, the spiritual center of the western world. It was constructed with only one way in and one way out.

Like a fortress.

The metaphor was a good one. There was a battle

41

raging, and much of the fighting was directed from inside the walls of this city. What, then, did that make him? A soldier? That is what his superiors would have liked him to think, but he knew it was too grand a term.

Trash collector is more like it, he thought. Another good metaphor, one that would annoy his higher-ups. That thought pleased him, and he found himself smiling for the first time today.

He stepped past the gates. Inside the city, there was a different air. The buildings were ancient, even by Italian standards. Most of the one square mile of the Vatican had not changed in decades, some of it not for centuries.

"Van Helsing!" a voice called out, and he turned his head to see Carl approaching, his plain brown friar's robes billowing around him. Carl's blond hair was always a mess, its shape marked by the tendency to turn up at the sides. And he never had less than a day's growth on his face. Of course, the friar was both a religious man and . . . a what? Scientist? Inventor? Scholar? He was all of those things, his mind never on fewer than three matters at once. It was no wonder he was less than meticulous in his grooming.

"Still in one piece?" Carl asked. His tone was light, but Van Helsing recognized the concern there.

"It's still early."

"Your equipment?"

"We're going to need some replacements," Van Helsing replied. He didn't have to look at Carl to know that the man was eyeing him in disapproval.

"Did you bring *anything* back?"

Van Helsing glared at him instead of answering.

"I make these things for you to help you on your assignments," the friar began complaining. "Perhaps if you showed them a bit more respect—"

"I'm afraid that *assignments* can be very tough on your toys." Carl was not exactly a friend, but he was as close to one as Van Helsing had had in the last seven years. Plus, the two men had a professional relationship that Van Helsing appreciated. Carl provided him with the tools he needed to do his work.

The friar shrugged. "It's just as well; I've made some improvements anyway. I can show you—"

Van Helsing waved him off with a hand. "Later."

Carl nodded and said, "The cardinal wants to see you in his office."

"That will have to wait until later as well." He was looking forward to cleaning up and having his first good night's sleep in days.

"The cardinal wants to see you *now.*"

He cursed inwardly but said nothing. A short time later, he and Carl approached the Vatican Palace—more of a collection of connected buildings that represented a number of periods in the Vatican's long history. The palace held more than a thousand rooms, including the residence for the pope himself and offices for much of the Church's hierarchy. It was also home to the Vatican library, numerous museums, archives, and other sections whose purpose he could only guess at.

Carl walked Van Helsing as far as the door and then left him. Though it was still early, there were people scurrying about. All of them managed to be looking somewhere else when he strode down the marble floor. Clearly, they all feared him—his very name struck terror throughout the land—but perhaps it went even beyond that. Maybe they simply did not want to associate with the man who collected the trash—perhaps especially *their* trash.

The palace was a maze and it was easy to get lost inside, but Van Helsing knew the way and soon was standing outside of the cardinal's offices. He was met and escorted the rest of the way. After he was announced, he was led into Cardinal Jinette's inner office.

His Eminence was, of course, in his red satin robes, and Van Helsing realized that he had never seen the man wear anything else. Though he must have been at least fifty, the cardinal's thinning hair was still brown, with hardly a trace of gray. At the moment, his intense gaze was leveled squarely at Van Helsing. "Your assignment is complete?"

His only reply was a raised eyebrow.

"Of course. You *rarely* fail us." The rebuke was clear in Jinette's voice.

Van Helsing didn't take the bait. "It's good to be appreciated," he said. "Now, if that's all, I will be—"

"We have another assignment for you."

"You can tell me about it in the morning." Van Helsing turned to go.

"You leave immediately."

He turned back to the cardinal and waited stonily.

"It's a very strange case, one you're already quite

familiar with: Doctor Jekyll has moved his operation from London to Paris," the cardinal said.

Van Helsing's throat caught at the sound of that name. Dr. Jekyll had developed a chemical formula that had transformed him into the monstrous alter ego Mr. Hyde. He had killed a number of people already—back in London, Van Helsing had almost succeeded in bringing Hyde's reign of terror to an end, having injured the creature, who had then disappeared. It had been a rare failure for Van Helsing, but he learned from his mistakes.

"As you know, Mr. Hyde is an . . . ," the cardinal began.

"Abomination," Van Helsing finished.

"Your horse is already waiting for you outside, packed up with everything you need. And take precautions that you are not recognized. You have achieved a level of . . . renown in France." Then the cardinal looked down at the papers on his desk and began writing. Van Helsing recognized the gesture; he was being dismissed, but he continued standing there.

After a few seconds the cardinal looked up, cross. "Is there a problem?"

Van Helsing lifted his hands. "If it's all right, *Your Eminence*, I'll take a few minutes to *wash the blood off.*" For a long moment, neither man spoke; then Cardinal Jinette went back to his writing.

The Vatican's very special agent headed for his own quarters, which were in a nearby complex. He moved quickly: there was much work to be done and not a minute to waste.

3

Transylvania, Romania

THE DEEP FOREST WAS ALREADY COOL WITH THE CHILL OF fall, hinting at the bite of winter. In the misty gloom and fading moonlight, the man was bound to the sacrificial post, his hands tied over his head. He flexed against his bonds, but gave no struggle.

An unusual silence had descended on the forest—even the early morning mountain winds could barely be heard rustling through the branches.

If the man felt a growing anxiety, he gave no apparent sign, scanning the trees around him, boldly prepared to meet his fate.

It was almost time.

Snap. A twig fell from above. The rustle of leaves. Remarkably small indications considering what they heralded.

More noise. The creak of a tree.

The man's head suddenly craned upward.

Even from thirty feet below, the creature appeared remarkably agile for something with its great mass and its height of more than seven feet. Using its very large and sharp claws, the werewolf clung nearly horizontally to the bark of the tree. It took a moment to study its prey, with terrible cunning in its eyes.

The man remained alert but steady and defiant, remarkably so for someone facing one of the most dangerous creatures on Earth.

"Come on. Dracula's unleashed you for a reason," he challenged.

The name of the creature's master spoken aloud seemed to spur it to action. Snarling viciously through its awful, oversize canines, it leaped down from its perch, eager to tear its helpless victim to shreds.

Only a split second left and no margin for error. Prince Velkan of the proud Valerious quickly ripped loose of his bindings as the hunt came full circle. The blood and meat that had been set out as bait already worked the werewolf into a frenzy . . . though it had been momentarily lulled by the sacrificial post. Some of the more superstitious villagers still used such posts to make offerings—human sacrifices to quell the monsters' hunger for blood. Now the tradition came in handy.

Turning, Velkan reached up and vaulted to the top of the post the instant before the werewolf slammed into it. Velkan lunged to grab the vine hanging above him, even as one of his men on the ground threw a lever. Instantly the vine pulled Velkan up and away from the monster toward safety.

This was perhaps the most critical part of the hunt: when Velkan would be closest to the creature and in the most danger. There were merely a dozen feet between the two when the moving vine came to a halt.

Down below, hiding under the cover of the brush, Velkan's beloved sister, Anna, felt the blood drain from her face as she caught her brother's eyes. Just as she had dreaded, something had gone horribly wrong during their family's most important work. Despite that Velkan always took the greatest risks and had never once faltered, there were always too many complications and too many opportunities for mistakes during the hunt.

Now Velkan was inches away from certain death.

The world seemed to shrink around her. For a moment, there was only herself, her brother, and the creature. There were also sounds: rustling, a struggle of some kind. Then one of their men bellowed in panic, "It's stuck! It's stuck!" But all distractions were pushed out of her mind by a single overriding concern: Her brother was in trouble.

With no conscious effort on her part, she reached for her sword and drew it. Hands were grabbing her. "No! Anna! It will kill you!"

She tore free and exclaimed, "That's my brother out there!" Looking out into the clearing, she saw the beast snarling up at Velkan. They had surprised it and that had made it a bit more cautious. But they had also angered it, and that made it even more dangerous.

Anna charged out of the bushes, holding her sword in front of her. The beast's eyes were instantly on her, and so were her brother's. "Anna! No!" Velkan shouted. She ignored him—Anna had seen too many people close to her die, and she wasn't about to let Velkan become the next on that list. There were only the two of them left since their father had disappeared. Her own death had seemed inevitable to her for years now. She would do whatever she could while she lived, but in the end, Velkan would be the last of the family Valerious.

She was covering the distance between them quickly and raised her blade higher. She was glad to see the doubt on the creature's face. It could not decide whether to turn to face her or to continue its attack on Velkan. A moment later, it leaped off the post in Anna's direction.

Steeling herself, she lifted her weapon and prepared to strike. She might not be able to defeat the creature, but she would fight it to the end . . . and perhaps she could weaken it enough to give Velkan an advantage.

She heard the werewolf's roar as it sailed through the air. It landed hard on the ground just a few feet in front of her . . . and kept falling, into the hidden trap, the exact location of which even Anna had forgotten in the heat of the moment.

Anna gave a silent thanks and heard the sound of

an ax striking the rope. A huge iron cage seemed to rip itself from the ground in front and under her as well.

She jumped backward, turning in the air and landing perfectly, watching as the cage was pulled up higher. Still hanging on to the vine, Velkan drew his silver revolver as the roof of the cage sprang shut, trapping the werewolf inside—at least for now.

Velkan wouldn't miss that shot at fifty yards, and there was much less than that separating him from the monster. As he readied to fire down into the cage, it slammed into Velkan on its way up into the trees. The revolver went flying, and Velkan was stuck on top of the cage, a situation that Anna herself had narrowly avoided. Now her brother and the trap were racing straight up into the huge trees.

Far above ground, it slammed to a stop. Velkan dove off and landed on a nearby branch, safe for the moment. Anna found no relief. Two things had gone wrong on the hunt already; it was a miracle they had survived the first one, and it seemed impossible that the werewolf would grant them the chance to survive the second.

Immediately, the creature started to thrash inside the cage, causing it to crash back and forth.

The iron was strong, but it would not hold for long. As if on cue, one of the ropes holding the cage snapped. Then another.

"My gun! My gun!" Velkan called out, the worry

in his voice frightening Anna more than anything that had happened so far. She desperately began to search the brush around her. The four men around her fired their rifles up into the trees—a foolish venture. If they succeeded in hitting the creature, they would only enrage it.

"No! Find Velkan's gun! It has to be the silver bullets!" she shouted.

She heard another rope snap but didn't dare look up. The cage was swinging wildly now. Once the werewolf was free, the hunt would be over for all of them.

Anna concentrated on the task at hand. Finally she saw the revolver lying on the far side of the clearing. Even as she moved, she heard the final snap, and the cage crashed down just a few feet in front of her.

An instant later, the werewolf burst out of its smashed prison, and Anna saw the anger blazing in its horrible yellow eyes.

Her reaction was automatic and came from a place deeper and older than even her family's traditions and training.

She ran for her life.

She did not have to look back to know that the werewolf was right on her heels. It would not rest until she was dead. Her only satisfaction came from knowing that she was giving Velkan precious seconds to recover.

Anna knew these woods well—she would run out of ground even before the creature reached her.

Scrambling out of the forest, she entered a few yards of clearing.

Her body was so aware of the danger behind her that she barely stopped herself before she went over the cliff—the edge of the Transylvanian Plateau, twelve hundred feet up. Looking down, she could not even see the bottom through the mist.

Spinning around, Anna decided to sprint back to the trees. Better to face her enemy than let herself be chased into the void. It seemed like a good idea . . . until she saw brush thrown into the air. The werewolf was *very* angry.

Anna froze.

She had imagined her death a thousand times. Each time she had died bravely, fighting—not standing helpless while she waited for the end. Yet, Anna now found that she could not move.

The werewolf emerged, plunging out of the bushes and straight at her. All she could do was face the end with dignity.

Then the impossible happened.

Something shoved roughly at her from one side. No, not something: *someone.* Velkan.

Anna flew out of harm's way and hit the ground. Spinning, she saw her brother standing steadfast. Velkan raised his gun and fired. The great creature howled in pain but managed to lunge forward, biting into Velkan's shoulder and throwing him backward . . .

. . . into the abyss.

Her mind could not accept what she had just seen.

It wasn't possible. Velkan was the strong one with the real courage. He was the one who was supposed to survive, the one who would finish their family's work . . . Father's . . . Mother's . . .

And she owed her brother her own life, twice now. He could not leave her, not with that debt unpaid. Anna stepped to the edge of the cliff, expecting Velkan to be hanging on to a bush or a root. He would pull himself up and smile at her—that self-satisfied grin that made her crazy.

Anna looked over the side and saw only the rough edge of the cliff wall and the mist below it.

"Velkan . . . ," she whispered.

There was a noise behind her and Anna whirled. There it was: the werewolf, lying in the bushes. Anna grabbed the gun lying on the ground, prepared to finish her brother's work. But the creature began to ripple and shift, then to shrink, finally shedding its fur like a second skin and disappearing before her eyes.

Seconds later, the creature was gone, replaced by an old man in the last moments of his life. Anna could see the bullet hole in his chest. Velkan had not missed.

"Thank you," the old man whispered.

You killed my brother, she thought. *No, not you: that thing you became.*

He gave a thin smile. "I am free from Dracula's awful grip." With the last of his dying energy, he grabbed Anna's ankle. When he spoke next, his voice held new strength. "But now you must stop him! . . . He has a terrible secret. . . . He has . . . he has . . . !"

He exhaled a final time and was still. Anna stared down at him and then turned to look over the cliff again. When the tears came, she was powerless to fight them.

4

Paris, France

AS HE WALKED THE STREETS, VAN HELSING MADE SURE THE mask covering the bottom half of his face was secure. It would not do to attract attention now. That was easy enough this late on a rainy night with few people on the streets—less than usual, he was certain, because of the recent . . . *trouble*. His wide-brimmed hat covered much of what his mask did not. Someone would have to get very close to him to see his eyes—and he didn't intend to let that happen. His long and flowing dark cloak hid the shape of his body, completing the disguise. It had the additional advantage of holding all of his field equipment.

Paris felt somewhat familiar, as if he had spent considerable time here, but of course he had no memory of ever visiting it before his brief trips over the last few years. He no longer questioned that sort of déjà vu. He was reasonably certain that he himself was not French. Even if there were answers for him in this city, he did not think he would find them tonight.

He caught sight of a very large half-built iron tower in the background. *That's new,* a voice inside of him said. He knew that voice well: It was that of another life he could not remember, one that taunted him with glimpses of a past unknown.

Dancing shadows played across a dog-eared poster slapped on a wall illuminated by gaslight, seeming to animate the heavy black letters that screamed AVIS DE RECHERCHE! (WANTED!) And for 2,000 francs, no less. Similar signs peppered the city, and Van Helsing had to admit that the likeness of him was a good one. That captured the French psyche perfectly for him: They got the fine details right, but still managed to entirely miss the most important points. They thought *he* was the enemy? If they only knew about the real dangers out there, they would drop their baguettes and run for the hills.

A high-pitched, blood-curdling scream pierced the night. He hated to admit it, but the cardinal was right: He *had* been needed here.

Reaching out, he pulled down the poster, crumpling it in his hand. Well, at least the French *appreciated* his efforts on their behalf. He walked with new purpose, heading for the source of trouble.

It did not take long for him to find her. She lay in the great stone courtyard in front of the Cathedral of Notre Dame. She was dead, no doubt of that. He quickly scanned her broken body to make certain that this was the work of . . . his assignment. On the ground next to her, something small was burning.

Reaching down, he picked up a smoldering cigar stub covered with saliva. There it was, a sound, something that didn't belong in this world. His prey was nearby. He quickly searched the cathedral with his eyes. There was enough moonlight that he could trace the individual spires and gables of the great building.

He had never been this close to the cathedral before, at least not that he could remember. Notre Dame was beautiful, a tremendous achievement in both design and construction. It had two large bell towers that rose up on each side, flanking a single enormous stained-glass window high up near the center of the building. Begun in the twelfth century, it was one of the truly magnificent works of man. And now lying dead in front of it was the work of a monster.

There. A shadowy figure was scaling the sheer wall halfway up the side of the building, and then disappeared over a railing. Van Helsing headed for the front door of the cathedral.

Once inside, he started up the stairs. Following his ears, he made his way to the north bell tower. Stepping up into the belfry, he saw a dark and dusty room filled with religious statuary and relics. The past was in here for many . . . but not for him. Here, all he would find was his assignment.

He kept his senses sharp as he passed the massive church bell. Moonlight shone through the windows, but there were many gloomy corners and shadows in the large room. Then he both heard and felt the danger nearby.

Van Helsing froze, every part of him poised and ready. The very large figure dropped in front of him, hanging upside down from the rafters, snarling gutturally. The muscular creature was at least nine feet tall and looked like a man with all of his finer qualities removed, his hair matted, his brow exaggerated, his skin hairy, sallow, and rough, the large jowls with graying muttonchops and mouth that dripped saliva.

Mr. Hyde wore no clothing save a pair of torn trousers. The monster would have looked completely animal-like but for the burning cigar clamped between his rotting teeth, the smell of which did little to hide the stench of death and decay that emanated from him. Hyde's malice was as palpable as a chill.

Van Helsing had no doubt that he was looking into the face of evil—not the theoretical evil of religious discussion, but the reality of it. An evil that took life for pleasure, for sport, its most recent victim lying on the pavement outside. An evil that would kill with as little hesitation as a normal man would have a meal. In fact, Mr. Hyde would likely combine the two activities if he could.

Van Helsing took a step back. "Evening," he said, keeping his voice neutral.

The creature looked him over and answered in a rough growl, "You're a big one. You'll be hard to digest."

"I'd hate to be such a nuisance." He was surprised at the creature's attempt at humor. Mr. Hyde had once been Dr. Jekyll, a renowned physician. How much of the doctor survived inside that corrupt form? He immediately pushed the thought aside; it merely made his work harder, and he could not afford distraction.

Hyde somersaulted down and nimbly landed on his gnarled feet. Van Helsing looked him over, reminding himself not to underestimate him as a foe.

"I missed you in London," Van Helsing remarked.

Hyde gave him an unpleasant smile and said, "No, you didn't." He lifted up his huge arm to show three cauterized bullet holes that Van Helsing had blown straight through the creature's biceps.

"You got me good," Hyde seethed, circling him, looking more predator than man. Van Helsing matched his movements.

There was a single formality to be performed before he finished the job begun in London. "Dr. Jekyll, you are wanted by the Knights of the Holy Order—"

"It's Mr. Hyde now."

He ignored the interruption. Though he doubted there was anything left of the doctor in the thing in front of him, whatever was still Jekyll deserved to hear the charges against him. "—for the murder of twelve men, six women—"

Hyde smiled again and finished, "—four children, three goats, and a rather nasty massacre of poultry." The monster sized him up before declaring, "So you're the great Van Helsing." Hyde blew a large smoke ring in his direction, as if to taunt him. He ignored it.

"You are a deranged psychopath." As if to prove Van Helsing's statement correct, Hyde took his hot cigar out of his mouth and crushed the glowing end on his palm. Van Helsing winced inside but kept his expression steady. Hyde didn't even flinch.

"We all have our little problems," the creature opined.

It was time. Soon all pretense would fall away and this matter would be settled. There was a rhythm to these encounters, and Van Helsing recognized the signs. He readied his body and his mind, calling on all of his training and his instincts. "My superiors would like for me to take you alive, so that they may extricate your better half."

"They would, would they?" Hyde snarled back.

"Personally, I'd rather just kill you and call it a day." That much was true; he didn't see any hope for Dr. Jekyll.

"Let's make it your decision, shall we?" Hyde just laughed.

When the creature moved, it was quick and sudden. He lashed out with one of his oversize hands, catching his nemesis in the face and slamming him back into the wall behind him.

Van Helsing calmly wiped the blood off of his mouth. "Good. We're in agreement, then."

Taking a creature like Mr. Hyde in was much riskier than simply killing him. There was too great a danger of him escaping to murder again. And then there was the problem of extricating Jekyll from this monster— for the people who did that work, the process was at least as hazardous as Van Helsing's own.

Still, the cardinal had insisted that he make the attempt to reach the doctor and give him the chance. Van Helsing had done that much. Now it was time to do *his* work: to collect this trash.

In one swift movement he reached into his cape, drawing the revolvers holstered on each hip. The reports thundered in the bell tower as the powerful weapons jumped in his hands.

He stood his ground, waiting for the smoke from the pistols to clear. When it did, Hyde was not there. Well, he *was* almost supernaturally fast. Van Helsing holstered his guns, anticipating the enemy's next move.

Hyde suddenly charged at him out of the shadows. Reaching into his cloak again, Van Helsing grasped the circular blades decorated with Chinese inscriptions—one of the Vatican's newer inventions. Stepping out of Hyde's way, he pivoted on his feet and lashed out with the blades, cutting the creature across the ribs as he passed.

Howling in pain, Hyde continued forward several steps until he crashed into the huge church bell, which clanged loudly from the impact. Hyde managed to stay on his feet, holding his ears and screaming out, "The bell! The *bell!*"

Van Helsing started to spin the spring-loaded blades in his hands. They turned quickly against their handles, building up more and more speed until they were just blurs.

Hyde's eyes focused on the blades. In response, he grabbed the enormous bell with both hands, tearing it from its yoke in a feat of incredible strength even for something his size. Before Van Helsing could move, he saw the bell coming toward him.

That was it—his final miscalculation. Van Helsing had skills and training that made him a match for anyone of this world and many who belonged in the next. But he was only flesh and blood. As the bell came down on him, he would be instantly crushed. At least it would be quick.

And then everything went dark, though the killing blow never came. Suddenly he realized why: Hyde had used the bell to trap him instead. The creature was toying with Van Helsing, like a cat playing with a helpless mouse.

Hyde laughed at his own cleverness—the esteemed Van Helsing was now trapped like a bug in a jar. For all of his reputation, he had been relatively easy prey . . . not much harder than all the others. Hyde's next meal would indeed be savored like no other before it.

A muted buzzing came from inside the bell—the unmistakable sound of wood being sawed through. The monster's grin faded and was replaced with pure rage at this latest trickery.

Van Helsing would never escape. Reaching out with his gigantic arms, Hyde hoisted the tremendously heavy bell over his head—a feat not lost on someone who would have had difficulty even ringing it in his previous incarnation . . . as that weakling Jekyll.

He reveled in his strength and power, even as he spied the circular hole that his nemesis had cut into the floor. *Gone!*

The buzzing sound came again, but this time from above. Caught by surprise, Hyde instinctively looked up. Van Helsing was waiting inside the bell, a smile on the hateful man's face.

Before the monster could even react, Van Helsing slashed downward. The circular blade met Hyde's raised left arm, and a second later the severed limb was on the floor, flailing for a few moments, as if unwilling to accept its fate.

Howling in pain, Hyde dropped the bell with a crash, splintering the wood floor as Van Helsing rolled free of his temporary prison.

"I'll bet that was upsetting," Van Helsing remarked.

This won't take long now, he thought, preparing to jump down and end this battle, but something caught his attention. The severed arm stopped moving, as if the life and malice inside had vanished. In front of Van Helsing's eyes, it transformed from the powerful limb of an evil monster into the thin, spindly arm of a harmless old man.

He was frozen by the sight. Perhaps the doctor was in there somewhere, too overwhelmed by the malicious power of Hyde to break free.

The creature made the most of Van Helsing's moment of distraction and with a fierce lunge, grabbed him with its remaining arm, throwing him straight up. Van Helsing felt himself flying toward the ceiling and then crashing through it.

The cool night air assaulted his senses as he came down onto the deck, a cloud of unconsciousness looming and threatening to overwhelm him.

Shaking his head, he tried to get up. He had to. Hyde was nearby, he could sense it. . . .

Too late. Van Helsing was yanked up by the back of his collar. He shook his head again and breathed deeply, feeling the chill reviving him.

"I think you'll find the view up here rather spectacular," he heard the creature laugh.

They were at the edge of the tower, and Hyde lifted him so that they were face-to-face. Van Helsing could smell the stink of the monster's last meal on his breath; it reeked of rotting flesh. Van Helsing decided not to speculate on what Hyde had eaten.

The abomination smiled at him, and Van Helsing searched his face for any sign of humanity. He saw none.

"Been a pleasure knowing you," Hyde reflected, and Van Helsing was cast into open space, hurtling toward the ground below. Completely alert and without even thinking, he drew the grappling gun holstered at his side, aimed, and fired. The hook shot out, its tether trailing behind it. Van Helsing sensed the earth rushing up beneath him and knew that it would be close—very close.

The grappling hook blew right through Hyde's stomach. He fell back, out of Van Helsing's sight, and the hook's line went taut. Van Helsing held on to the gun with both hands and felt himself snap to a halt. Looking down for the first time, he realized that he was hanging just two feet above the cobblestones.

The line suddenly went slack, and Van Helsing crumpled to the ground. Looking up, he saw that the creature was teetering on a ledge, barely keeping himself from falling over. The grappling line had gone straight through him, and the barbed steel on the end of the hook would make certain that it did not come out easily.

Getting to his feet, Van Helsing grabbed the tether and gave it a quick, solid yank. He watched as Hyde tipped forward. The monster immediately pin-wheeled backward with his single arm, and then with all of his might threw himself out of view.

Still holding on to his grappling gun, Van Helsing was pulled up off the ground. There was a distant crash; Hyde had plummeted through the roof of the church. Before he could let go of the gun, Van Helsing flew toward the top of the tower as Hyde fell. On his way up, he witnessed the monster smashing through the great stained-glass window of Notre Dame, which exploded outward, a deadly hailstorm of multicolored shards raining down on the court-yard.

Miraculously, Van Helsing landed a moment later, hard but on his feet, at the top of the tower. Peering over the edge, he saw the last seconds of Hyde's descent. The creature seemed to ripple and shrink as he struck the cobblestones.

Mr. Hyde was dead. And he had died a man, not a monster.

Van Helsing had been very lucky more than once during the course of this encounter, but he felt neither victorious nor fortunate. Instead a hollow sadness opened up within him.

The fact that the monster was dead gave him no comfort: the man, Dr. Jekyll, *had* been in there all along. Had the doctor fought against the darkness of Mr. Hyde? From what Van Helsing knew of the case, the doctor created the formula that had transformed him as part of his medical research. He had used it on himself, once and then again, with greater and greater frequency—until there was no turning back.

How had it felt for Jekyll to lose his humanity, step by step, dose by dose until there was no man left at all . . . just a monster? Did he know what was happening at the beginning of his journey? How had he felt when he took those first steps toward the abyss?

Van Helsing was afraid that he already knew the answer. He made the sign of the cross. "God rest your soul. . . ."

People were gathering, pointing up at him.

"Van Helsing! . . . It's Van Helsing!" someone in the small crowd called out.

He recognized the sergeant of the gendarmes,

who raised an angry fist and screamed in French, *"Van Helsing, you murderer!"*

Other figures were running to the scene and would be coming up the stairs. He turned around and headed for the rear of the tower. He could be on the ground in seconds with his grappling hook, but it was gone now, buried inside the belly of a dead old man outside.

Van Helsing started climbing down and was making his final leap to the street when he heard the first voices from above. Disappearing into the shadows, he soon came face-to-face with two men who had run outside of a pub to see the commotion.

Skidding to a stop in front of them, Van Helsing saw the flash of recognition in their eyes. *"Vous!"* one of them exclaimed, holding out a finger in accusation.

Reflexively, Van Helsing drew a pistol and pointed it at the larger of the two men. He wouldn't use it unless he had to, but he had had it with the French today. Without thinking, he cocked the hammer and prepared to shoot.

A boy stepped out from behind the man Van Helsing was aiming at. It was obvious that he was the child's father.

Time stopped as they looked at Van Helsing. His heart dropped into his stomach and he felt as though he were teetering on the edge of a precipice. As quickly as he could, he uncocked and holstered the weapon.

Turning away, Van Helsing made his way down the narrow lane toward his horse, taking measures to ensure that anyone following him would lose the trail. He knew he didn't need to worry that the two men and the child had seen him.

There had been fear in their eyes.

5

THREE DAYS LATER, AT DAWN, VAN HELSING RODE INTO
Rome, a dark-cloaked figure on a black stallion. He
made his way to the Vatican and passed the great
gates, riding hard across the enormous Piazza San
Pietro, the tremendous open space in front of St.
Peter's Basilica. He was surrounded by history again,
by the past. The bells chimed as he passed the two
great fountains and the two semicircular rows of
columns that surrounded the large open space. The
columns led to and seemed to guard the basilica as
they had for centuries.

St. Peter's was both the oldest and greatest church
in all of Christendom. One of Jesus Christ's apostles,
St. Peter, had suffered Christ's fate on earth and was
crucified, though he had insisted on an inverted
cross in his humility. According to Church lore, the
great basilica was built on the site of Peter's burial—
on his very blood.

Van Helsing always felt a moment of reverence

whenever he approached the church. There was the weight of the centuries the structure had endured, the sheer size and beauty of the place, and something else: a sense that one of the largest buildings in the world stood for something even greater than itself.

Reaching the stairs in the front of the church, Van Helsing drew his horse to a halt and dismounted, handing the reins to the man who waited for him. Then he stepped into the church and strode across the marble floor. The light inside the building came from the clerestories, the upper portion of the outer walls that held the stained-glass windows. It was warm, colorful, meant to give worshippers a sense of the wonder of creation and of peace. At the moment, Van Helsing felt neither.

The church was built in the shape of a cross, at the center of which was the great dome created by Michelangelo himself. The structure was more than seven hundred feet deep, and it took Van Helsing some time to reach his destination. As he walked, he heard the chanting of monks.

In the past, the Gregorian chants had quieted his mind, and he had found rare moments of peace inside this building. However, this time the sounds grated on his ears, and the very structure seemed to judge him and find him wanting.

Van Helsing reached an ornate confessional and stepped inside. Falling to one knee, he said, "Bless me, Father, for I have sinned." He gritted his teeth and steeled himself for what would come next. A tiny partition door slid down in front of him, and he could see a figure behind the wooden mesh there.

The voice that spoke to him was angry, indignant, and disappointed—a tone that was unique to Cardinal Jinette. "You shattered the Rose Window!"

"Not to split hairs, sir, but it was Mr. Hyde that did the shattering."

Ignoring him, the cardinal continued to rant: "Built in the thirteenth century—over six hundred years old! I wish you a week in hell for that!"

"It would be a nice reprieve," Van Helsing replied, his voice defiant.

"Don't get me wrong: Your results are unquestionable, but your methods draw far too much attention. Wanted posters? We are not pleased." The cardinal was now merely exasperated.

Van Helsing felt his own frustration rising. "You think I like being the most wanted man in Europe? Why don't you and the Order do something about it?"

The cardinal leaned in and lowered his voice. "You know why: because *we* do not exist."

"Then neither do I." He rarely won an argument with the cardinal, and though this was a small point, it felt like a great victory. Van Helsing got to his feet and turned to go when he heard a click from the cardinal's side. Immediately, bolts on his door slid into place. His Eminence moved closer, his voice tight and deadly serious.

"When we found you crawling up the steps of this

church, bloodied and half dead, it was clear to all of us that you had been sent to do God's work."

"Why can't He do it Himself?" Van Helsing shot back.

"Don't blaspheme! You already lost your memory as a penance for past sins."

There was a second click as the cardinal pulled another lever. A series of gears started working and the back walls of both confessional booths slid away, revealing a secret staircase. "If you wish to recover it, I suggest you continue to heed the call."

Van Helsing sighed. As also often happened during these encounters with the cardinal, he had won a small victory but lost the war. The two men walked down the stairs in silence, and a few seconds later they entered the underground armory beneath the confessional. It was enormous, but still only a small part of the subterranean universe that was hidden under the great basilica.

The armory was, as usual, bustling with action, with the steam of the blast furnaces filling the air. Van Helsing could feel the heat of the fires, which felt to him like the flames of God's own wrath. He noted the Jewish rabbis working the billows and Hindu priests stoking the fires as Muslim imams hammered red-hot scimitars on anvils.

There *was* a war going on. A few days before, Van Helsing had been on the front line; now he was back at headquarters, awaiting his orders.

As they walked, Cardinal Jinette intoned a familiar lecture: "Governments and empires come and go, but we have kept mankind safe since time immemorial. We are the last defense against evil—an evil that the rest of mankind has no idea even exists."

Van Helsing knew this speech by heart, having heard it often. The cardinal had the need to repeat it from time to time, and, Van Helsing had to admit, there were times when he needed to hear it. Evil did exist—he had seen too much in the last seven years to deny it. In that time, he had studied, fought, and defeated it.

Jinette spoke the truth, but there were things he did not say and perhaps he could not understand: that in Van Helsing's work, victory came at a price. A war was being waged and the cardinal was a general who couldn't understand the cost paid by his foot soldiers. "To you, these monsters are evil beings to be vanquished," Van Helsing observed, "but I'm the one left standing there when they die and become the men they were."

Jinette was quiet for a moment. When he finally spoke, his tone was gentle. "For you, my good son, this is all a test of faith. That is why you have no idea of who you are or where you come from." Van Helsing looked closely at the cardinal, waiting for something . . . an answer, perhaps. "Say you met God, and he set you on a task," the cardinal continued. "You would have no fear because you would know that God was with you. But if your memory of meeting God were lost, then every day would be a test of faith."

Not an answer, exactly—at least, not the kind that

Van Helsing was looking for. How much did the cardinal know about his past, his identity? More than he would say today, that much was certain.

But the cardinal was right: His faith was being tested. Somehow he hoped that knowing his past would make it easier for him to bear the terrible price of his work, or perhaps leave it behind. A weariness descended on him and weighed on more than his body.

The cardinal snapped his fingers and the light around them dimmed. One of the clerics activated a slide projector. He clicked the machine and the images changed, showing the way from Rome to lands in Eastern Europe. Van Helsing knew what was coming. The cardinal was about to ask something of him. It would be too much, as usual, but he would expect Van Helsing to do it anyway. This time he might give the cardinal a surprise.

"We need you to go to the east, to the far side of Romania, an accursed land terrorized by all sorts of nightmarish creatures." Van Helsing knew the region; he had heard of what lurked in Romania's Carpathian Mountains, in the region known as Transylvania. An image of a man born of Eastern European royalty came up on the screen. The face was handsome, but there was something wrong with his eyes, Van Helsing noted. They were ice cold.

"How is your Romanian?" the cardinal asked.

Uncertainty must have showed on Van Helsing's face, because the cardinal asked, "You do speak Romanian?"

Van Helsing thought about it for a moment. "Yes."

"Good. The land is lorded over by a certain Count Dracula."

Van Helsing found that he was suddenly alert and studying the image with interest. He had heard of Dracula, of course, but he also had the strangest sense that he was seeing someone he knew.

The next picture was a painting of a nobleman from perhaps the fifteenth century. The man looked resolute, wearing a suit of armor covered in the sign of the cross. A name appeared on the bottom of the image: Valerious the Elder.

"Four hundred and fifty years ago, a Transylvanian knight named Valerious the Elder promised God that his family would never rest, not enter heaven, until they vanquished Dracula from their land. They have not succeeded, and they are running out of family."

More grainy images of family members appeared on the screen. There was a burly, robust-looking older man who looked like a king. There was the handsome face of a young man. "Boris Valerious, King of the Gypsies; he went missing almost a year ago. His son Velkan died just last week."

The image of a girl dressed all in black and seated on a horse replaced the young man. She was perhaps twenty and looked very beautiful—and very dangerous. She had long, dark hair that fell in rings halfway down her back. Though she was wearing tight black riding clothes, she had the look of someone who had seen battle. Her eyes were striking, piercing, and framed by thin, rounded eyebrows.

There was something wild about this woman, something in those eyes. Perhaps it was the Gypsy blood. "And the girl?" Van Helsing asked.

"Princess Anna, *the last of the Valerious*," the cardinal said pointedly. "If she is killed, nine generations of her family will never enter the gates of Saint Peter."

Suddenly the room flooded with light and the cardinal was facing Van Helsing. "For more than four centuries this family has held down our left flank. They gave up their lives, we cannot let them slip into purgatory."

"So you're sending *me* into hell."

"In a manner," Cardinal Jinette said simply. An old cleric stepped up and handed something to the cardinal, who held it up for Van Helsing. It was a torn piece of painted cloth encased in a strip of glass. The whole thing fit easily in the palm of his hand. "The old knight left this here four hundred years ago. We don't know its purpose, but he would not have left it lightly."

Van Helsing studied the piece. Painted on part of the cloth was an inscription. It was in Latin, *Deum lacessat ac inaum imbeat aperiri*, which the cardinal translated aloud: "In the name of God, open this door."

And then Van Helsing saw something that surprised him. In the corner of the cloth, there was the insignia of a dragon. He had not only seen it before, but the ring on his finger bore the same symbol, just as it had when the cardinal's men had first found him.

The cardinal witnessed the struggle that was playing out on Van Helsing's face and set a hand upon his special agent's arm in a fatherly gesture. "I think that in Transylvania you may find the answer you seek. . . ."

That was it. This time the cardinal's request came with an offer he knew Van Helsing would not refuse. One of these days he might find a way to say no to this man, but he knew it wouldn't be today.

A sense of urgency filled him, and he headed across the armory and straight through a large blast of steam.

A figure rushed up; Carl's brown robes were shaking as he ran. "There you are. Did you bring him back? Or did you kill him?"

Van Helsing didn't respond.

"You killed him, didn't you? That's why they get so annoyed. When they ask you to bring someone back, they don't mean as a corpse."

Van Helsing scowled and turned to Carl, who gave him only a small smile. "All right," he retreated. "You're in a mood. Well, come on, I've got a few things that will put the bit back in your mouth."

Again, Van Helsing found his interest rising. There was no denying that Carl was able to create things that were years ahead of the best weapon smiths of his time. Behind the friar Van Helsing noticed swords coming out of a flaming forge. Then again, sometimes the old, direct ways and arms were the best.

Carl was loud and indignant, when he said, "Any idiot can make a sword."

As if on cue, a large, beefy man wearing the robes of a Buddhist monk angrily stepped out from behind the forge, staring steely-eyed daggers at the friar.

"Sorry, Father!" Carl quickly led Van Helsing to a shelf. He grabbed some things and stuffed them into Van Helsing's arms, saying, "Rings of garlic, holy water, a wooden stake, a silver crucifix . . ."

Loud reports thundered over the din of the armory. Van Helsing turned and saw a large multibarreled firearm mounted on the floor. He had heard of this, the invention of a clever American named Gatling. The revolving rifle rapidly fired shot after shot, and Van Helsing saw he was looking into a window with a direct view of the future. He might also be seeing something he could use.

"Why can't I take one of those?"

Carl shot him an appraising look, staring at him as if he were a particularly dull child; it was a look that seemed to be the specialty of religious men. "You've never gone after vampires before, have you?"

Van Helsing shrugged. "Vampires, gargoyles, warlocks, they're all the same: *best when cooked well.*"

"They are not all the same. A vampire is nothing like a warlock. My granny could kill a warlock."

"Carl, you've never been out of the abbey. How do you know about vampires?"

There it was, that look again. "That's why they

make books." Of course—and the Vatican had without a doubt the largest library in the world. A small portion of that collection was on nearby shelves. Van Helsing saw volumes by Socrates, Copernicus, Da Vinci, and Galileo. Some of the greatest works written by the most brilliant thinkers in the history of man. And next to them were sticks of dynamite that seemed to be dripping sweat into vials.

Carl saw where he was looking and said, "Here's something new. Glycerine forty-eight." He stuck his pinky into one of the vials and flicked a drop of the dynamite sweat against a wall, which instantly burst into a large ball of flame. Several of the startled men around them yelled in unison, "Knock it off, Carl!"

Sheepish, Carl said, "Sorry! Sorry!" then turned back to Van Helsing. "The air around here is thick with envy."

In a casual movement that covered his obvious pride, Carl grabbed a strange-looking crossbow and handed it to Van Helsing. It was covered with iron pumps and copper tubes. "This is my latest invention." Carl was clearly pleased with himself. Van Helsing could see why: The weapon looked extremely effective.

"Now, this I like."

"Gas propelled, capable of catapulting bolts in rapid succession at tremendous velocity. Just pull the trigger and hold on," Carl said. Van Helsing studied the weapon with an appraising eye. Carl never exaggerated the value of his own creations; he didn't have to. Van Helsing adjusted the optical sight as

Carl continued: "I've heard stories coming out of Transylvania; trust me, you'll need this. A work of verifiable genius."

Van Helsing gave him a tight smile. "If you don't say so yourself."

After spending almost his whole life in the Vatican, among other religious men, Carl was immune to sarcasm and said plainly, "I did say so myself." Then he added without a hint of irony or humor, "I am a veritable cornucopia of talent."

Another contraption that Van Helsing had never seen before caught his eye, and he picked it up. "Did you invent this?"

Carl nodded. "I've been working on it for twelve years. It's compressed magma from Mount Vesuvius with pure alkali from the Gobi Desert. It's one of a kind."

That sounded impressive. "What's it for?"

"I have no idea, but I'm sure it will come in handy," Carl replied seriously, and started walking.

Van Helsing followed. "Twelve years and you don't know what it does?" Even for Carl, *that* was eccentric.

"I didn't say that. I said I don't know what it's *for*. What it *does* is create a light equal to the intensity of the sun."

"And this will come in handy how?"

Carl picked up two heavy cloth bags and handed them to Van Helsing. "I don't know. You could blind your enemies. Charbroil a herd of charging wildebeest. Use your imagination."

Typical, Van Helsing thought. Like most of the people at the headquarters of this war, Carl had no idea of what it was actually like in the field. And while Carl was brilliant, he had absolutely no idea of what life was like outside the Vatican. Well, it might be time to change all that. And if he was going after Dracula, Van Helsing knew he might need a little brilliance.

"No, Carl, I'm going to use *your* imagination. How's your Romanian?"

Confused, the friar shrugged and said, "Excellent, I think. I've never actually spoken it to a Romanian."

"That's why they make books," Van Helsing said. Carl nodded, squinting at Van Helsing, who added, "You're coming with me."

"The hell be damned if I am."

Van Helsing pointed with an accusing finger. "You *cursed.* Not very well, but you're a monk. You're not supposed to curse at all."

"Actually, I'm still just a friar, I can curse all I want . . . damn it."

"The cardinal has ordered you to keep me alive"—Van Helsing shoved the two cloth bags back into Carl's arms—"for as long as possible." With that, the Vatican's special agent headed through the forges that flamed and burned all around him.

I may be going into hell, but for once I'm not going alone.

Behind him, Carl's protest rang out: "But I'm not a field man!"

Aleera flew and dove between two mountain peaks. Marishka and Verona followed her. It took an effort for the other two brides to keep up. They were not as skilled in this or other, more important areas, such as pleasing their lord and master, Dracula.

In that arena Aleera also knew she was more capable. Still, the master had appetites that no one bride could quench, although Aleera often felt that she would like to try. And more importantly, for now, the Master's plan required the three of them. Once Dracula's dream was realized, well, anything was possible.

Flight was one of the few things besides serving Dracula that still gave Aleera pleasure. She liked the feeling of the air racing around her wings and the powerful body that was one of Dracula's greatest gifts to his brides. She also enjoyed looking at the living scurry around, knowing that she could have any one of them she wished at any time. In those moments, she knew what it must be like to be Dracula himself, with power over all who walked the earth.

She spied the village of Vaseria nestled in its valley and wished she could fly over the living there to let them see her. She needed to feed on their blood, but she also took advantage of their intoxicating fear. That sated another kind of hunger, one that was not as urgent as her lust for blood, but just as real.

Above the village square, Aleera chose a rooftop and brought herself to a halt above it. She took her human form as she landed, and saw Marishka and Verona doing the same next to her, their white wings transforming into white gowns.

"I am very, very excited about this," Aleera said, though she knew there was danger here, however slight. She preferred prey that looked at her in mute terror to that which fought back. No matter. These humans had no power to do her real harm.

"Why can't we just let the werewolf kill her?" Marishka asked.

Typical: lazy and cowardly, Aleera thought.

Verona gave Marishka a condescending look. "Never trust a man to do a woman's job."

6

VAN HELSING MADE SURE THE WIDE BRIM OF HIS HAT WAS covering his face, and he kept his head down as they entered the village. He glanced over at Carl to make sure the friar was doing the same. Of course, besides giving them a bit of anonymity, the hoods helped keep the two men warm. It was chilly, and there was a dusting of snow on the ground.

Vaseria was a fairly large town, at least by local standards. Its center had a number of small wooden buildings that were one or two stories high. Like much of the surrounding land, they had the look of age, having stood unchanged for decades.

The people of Vaseria looked positively vicious and he didn't need additional trouble on this trip; he figured he would have plenty soon enough from Count Dracula.

Even as they moved through the crowd, Carl kept up his constant chatter: ". . . So you can remember everything about your life from the last seven years, but nothing before that?"

"Not now, Carl."

"There must be something," Carl said, undeterred.

"I remember fighting the Romans at Masada," he said seriously.

He didn't have to see Carl's face to recognize the shock that was there. "That was seventy-three A.D . . . ?"

Van Helsing shrugged. "You asked."

Carl fell silent and Van Helsing looked over to see him peering nervously at the villagers, who were now giving the two newcomers suspicious glances. Carl would have noticed their reception immediately if he had been quiet for a moment. Not for the first time, Van Helsing questioned the wisdom of bringing the friar on this trip. Carl was often distracted, and he was proving to be a distraction for Van Helsing as well. His decision to bring him had been largely based on instinct, which had kept Van Helsing alive for seven years and had never led him astray.

At least until now. . . .

"What are we doing here?" Carl asked. "Why is it so important to kill this Dracula, anyway?"

"Because he's the son of the Devil," Van Helsing replied.

"I mean besides that."

"Because if we kill him, anything bitten by him or created by him will also die," Van Helsing explained.

"I mean besides that."

Van Helsing ignored the comment. Killing Dracula—that single act—might destroy more real monsters and more genuine evil than Van Helsing had managed to eradicate during his entire time in this line of work, and that was the only reason he needed. The cardinal would be very pleased; it would be a major victory in the Church's war, but Van Helsing had hopes that were far less grand. The mission might give him some answers about his own past, about why he remembered snatches of events from centuries before as if they had happened yesterday, when it was clearly impossible that he had even lived in those times. Ultimately, he hoped, destroying Dracula might actually bring him some peace.

A tall man in a large top hat appeared in front of them. Long, stringy blond hair and exaggerated cheekbones gave him a skeletal look. There was something odd about his eyes as well; they were large and manic. To Van Helsing he appeared to be an undertaker—one who took perhaps a trifle too much pleasure in his work. "Welcome to Transylvania," the man said in Romanian, the menace clear in his voice.

Immediately on guard, Van Helsing knew what would happen next; he had certainly seen it enough times. All the villagers who had been watching them took several steps in their direction and, as if by magic, produced knives, machetes, and pitchforks. In seconds, the newcomers were quickly surrounded.

Van Helsing could hear the change in Carl's

breathing and turned to see that the friar was terrified. It was, after all, his first angry mob and his first taste of what it was like "in the field." To his credit, he did not panic. "Is it always like this?" he asked, trying to sound nonchalant.

"Pretty much." Van Helsing scanned the crowd. Though they could be dangerous, a mob's mentality was almost childishly simple. Van Helsing had only one move available to him, and he would have to act fast. A group like this had no individual courage; their will came from their collective strength, directed by a single leader.

Van Helsing guessed that the man in the top hat was that leader, one who would have to be rendered powerless before the crowd came any closer. Though Van Helsing could probably survive even a direct assault by the group, he could not protect Carl at the same time.

He stayed his hand, though, since the villagers seemed unwilling to advance, almost as if they were waiting for instructions. Moments later a young woman appeared, and Van Helsing saw immediately who the real leader was. She took a place on top of the waist-high stone wall that ran around the well.

The girl . . .

He knew her. For a wild moment, Van Helsing thought she might be from his past, but then he remembered where he had seen her before: in the armory under St. Peter's. It was Anna—the one he was here to help.

The princess was dressed in black riding clothes

similar to the ones she had been wearing in her picture. "You! Let me see your faces!" It was a command, not a request.

Van Helsing was not very good at taking orders. He raised his head slightly and looked up at her from under the wide brim of his hat. "Why?" he asked.

"Because we don't trust strangers."

With good reason, in this land, Van Helsing thought. "I don't trust *anyone,*" he countered in Romanian, speaking it for the first time—at least, the first time he could remember.

The man in the top hat took out a measuring tape and started using it on Carl. "Strangers never last long here." He *was* the undertaker after all.

"Gentlemen, you will be disarmed," declared Anna. Several of the village men started to move closer. Van Helsing glared at them. The girl had changed the whole equation: This would not be a common encounter with an angry mob because she was no ordinary leader. This might actually be *interesting.*

"You can try," he said, keeping a challenge in his tone. The men stopped in their tracks, and Van Helsing could see their resolve wavering under his glare. *Maybe this will not be interesting after all,* he speculated.

"You refuse to obey our laws?" she asked.

"The laws of men mean little to me."

"Fine," Anna said. She turned to the crowd. "Kill them."

The villagers raised their weapons and started to close in.

"I'm here to help you," Van Helsing offered.

"I don't need any help." Even as she said it, Van Helsing saw movement behind her. Ignoring the crowd, he whipped Carl's newly designed crossbow from behind his back, taking only a fraction of a second to aim.

Anna saw his weapon pointed at her and ducked, which gave him a better view of the three giant white bats that were flying in formation right behind her. They were the size of men—or in this case women. Van Helsing could still make out three distinctly female faces on the creatures, with wingspans of perhaps twenty feet, and they had nasty-looking claws on each of their very powerful hands and feet.

Van Helsing had learned a few things about vampires since the cardinal had first given him his assignment. They had the strength of at least twenty men and the ability to take the form of demon bat creatures. What his studies hadn't told him was how vicious and deadly they looked. These were Dracula's brides, his undead servants. Van Helsing wondered what it would be like when he faced Dracula himself in mortal combat.

He fired three shots in rapid succession. Carl's invention launched the arrows with great speed and accuracy, but the creatures moved with unearthly speed and dodged the projectiles easily.

Now a number of the villagers were pointing up at the sky and yelling, *"Nosferatu!"*

All hell broke loose. The bats shot through the town center, ripping doors and shutters off their hinges, blowing over tables and chairs, and knocking people headlong on their faces. The bat creatures were trying to strike terror in the hearts of the villagers and, as far as Van Helsing could see, succeeding brilliantly. People were scurrying in panic.

Anna was still on top of the well. Her commanding voice boomed, "Everybody inside!" She was standing firm, higher up and more vulnerable than anyone else in the square. It was impressive but foolish.

Van Helsing kept firing, trying to get a bead on the brides. He chose his targets carefully, leading them to compensate for their great speed, but he wasn't able to score a single hit. Suddenly one of the bats swooped down, heading straight for Anna.

The princess saw it coming and dove off the well and right onto Van Helsing. Both of them crashed to the ground, with Anna now sprawled across him.

"Normally, I don't like women who throw themselves at me . . . ," he remarked, realizing that his crossbow was gone. He saw a flash of white and Anna was lifted off him by the bat, gripping the princess firmly in its talons as it beat its wings furiously. Van Helsing sprang to his feet and flung himself onto the top of the well. Leaping into the air, he grabbed Anna's legs as she was carried upward. He could feel the wind created by the creature's broad pounding wings.

"I thought you said you didn't need any help!" he shouted. Without warning, the vampire released Anna and the two tumbled back to earth from a height of less than a dozen feet.

For the second time, the princess landed on top of

Van Helsing, this time with her thighs straddling his face. He reached up, he grabbed her, and rolled her to the ground. "Stay here."

She pulled him back firmly and, with a similar movement, rolled *him* to the ground. "*You* stay here. They're trying to kill *me*." Then she bounded off him and ran. Van Helsing scrambled to his feet to go after her and spotted his crossbow lying in the dirt among the rushing villagers. Before he could make a dash for it, he saw two of the hideous bat women fly up over the rooftops.

One turned to the other and said, "Marishka, my dear, please kill the stranger."

"Love to."

Van Helsing did not have much time. Racing through the crowd, he grabbed his weapon and spun around. Two of the creatures whipped through the chaos, chasing Anna and tossing peasants out of their way. He ran for the princess and fired, throwing one of the creatures off balance. He aimed again and squeezed the trigger.

Nothing.

"Carl! I'm out!"

Immediately the friar pulled out a cartridge full of arrows and tossed it to Van Helsing, who caught it just as one of the bats swooped in. But there was no time to prepare a shot. Diving to the snow-covered dirt, he felt the breeze from its passage on the back of his neck. Looking up, he saw the clawed feet grab a luckless cow instead of him. The vampire lifted the heavy beast into the air and furiously pitched it through the second-story balcony of one of the nearby buildings.

Leaping up, Van Helsing slammed the cartridge into the crossbow and spun around to see Anna running across the far side of the square, one of the bats still on her trail. Shouldering his weapon, he launched multiple bolts in rapid fire. Dozens of arrows ripped into the storefronts all around the creature and Anna.

The princess catapulted over some crates as the monster swooped over her, just missing Anna with its groping claws and instead hoisted a fleeing man into the air. As the villager screamed in horror, Van Helsing could see a terrible smile on the creature's half-human face. "Be happy in the knowledge that your blood shall keep me beautiful," it said before biting into his throat. The undertaker cackled from behind a rack of coffins.

Anna popped up from behind the crates, which had dozens of arrows embedded in them. She was unhurt but flashed Van Helsing an angry look.

"Who are you trying to kill?!" she hissed.

A sudden silence fell over the entire square. Looking around, Dracula's brides were nowhere in sight, and all of the villagers were either indoors or hunkering down. Van Helsing shot the princess a questioning look. "The sun," she said, nodding upward. "Van Helsing!"

As a sliver of sun shone through the clouds, there was a loud splashing sound coming from the direction of the well. Slowly and by unspoken agreement,

Van Helsing and Anna inched toward it from opposite ends—Van Helsing with his crossbow at the ready and Anna wielding a scythe one of the villagers had dropped.

Closer . . . closer still . . . Van Helsing's and Anna's eyes met. As one, they looked over and down the well, both poised to strike.

The vampire barreled up and exploded out of the well's depths. Van Helsing was blown backward and watched as one of the brides took hold of Anna. Instantly back on his feet, he shouldered his crossbow and tried to track the creature, but Anna and the bat were already too far away.

Toying with the princess, the creature dragged Anna low across the rooftops, causing her riding boots to drag along the tops of the buildings. That was the creature's first mistake, Van Helsing realized: It had not simply killed Anna immediately.

The princess did not waste her opportunity. Pulling a switchblade out of her boot, she flicked it open and slashed at the bat creature's ankle. The monster shrieked and threw Anna into the air. Verona swooped in to grab her, and the princess's blade went flying.

Van Helsing fired a single arrow before it even registered that he had a good shot, hitting the bat in its clawed foot. Shrieking loudly, it dropped Anna, who fell a few feet to a steeply pitched roof.

As Anna tumbled down the incline of the roof, Van Helsing saw that she was about to go over the edge and then plummet forty feet straight to the ground. The princess did indeed roll off, but she surprised him by twisting around and grabbing on to the gutter. For a moment, she dangled precariously in the air.

She astonished him again by releasing her grip and flipping through the air to a tree. Launching herself off a limb, she landed catlike on her feet in a series of movements that was worthy of . . . well, worthy of him. This was someone he might not mind getting to know a little bit better.

Then Anna did exactly what he would have done in the same situation: She turned and ran like hell.

Suddenly, Carl yelled, "Van Helsing! Two o'clock!"

He pivoted around in time to see Marishka closing in on him. The crossbow came alive in his arms, firing a quick six bolts into the vampire. It spiraled wildly across the square and slammed straight through the side of a building.

Finally, a solid hit. This battle seemed to be turning. With any luck, they would be down to two vampires. It wasn't much, but at least it was progress.

Anna ran into a nearby house, slammed the door shut, and threw the bolt. The undead could not enter a home unless invited. For a little while at least she would be safe, with enough time to make a plan, ready herself, and come out fighting.

She turned and came face-to-face with Aleera, in her human form. She had gotten inside somehow. Hanging upside down from one of the ceiling beams, the vampire's long hair dangled to the ground. Casually she pulled her leg to her mouth and licked the bleeding ankle injured in Van Helsing's attack.

"Do you know how long I have wanted to kill you?" Aleera hissed. To Anna, the creature looked impossibly beautiful, but that was thin cover for the monster inside.

Anna backed away, fearing not her own death but the end of her family's centuries-long mission. She would not—could not—let her line end here.

First she would have to survive the next few minutes. Anna might be anyone's match, but the creature in front of her was both faster and stronger than any mortal, with the ability to summon powers against which Anna had no defense.

With blinding speed, Aleera sprang off the beam and landed between Anna and the door. The princess had no choice but to back into the living room as the vampire closed in for the kill. Anna desperately thought for a course of action.

And where the hell was that Van Helsing, who had waltzed into town saying that he wanted to help her? Where was he now, when she actually needed it?

"Don't play coy with me, Princess; you're just like all the other pretty little ancestors in your family, saying you want to destroy my master. But I know what lurks in your lusting heart," Aleera said. Then Anna saw it: black jealousy. Aleera had the Devil's own power and enough strength to snap her neck with a finger, but the creature was worried that

Anna might want to steal her evil master. It would have been humorous if the danger to her weren't so real and so immediate.

In an attempt to keep Aleera off balance, Anna countered, "I hope you have a heart, Aleera, because someday I'm going to drive a stake through it."

The vampire's casual uppercut caught Anna under the chin. The princess flew backward through a closed window. She heard and felt the glass shatter around her as she turned in the air to land on her feet outside. Before her brain even registered that she was still alive, Anna was already running down the adjoining alley.

With Carl right behind him, Van Helsing crept toward the building that the creature had crashed through. The friar was amazingly composed, given the circumstances, especially for his first time in the field. The people of this town had been dealing with the vampire threat their whole lives, but they still ran in terror at the first sight. Yet, Carl had stayed with Van Helsing and had been right there through it all.

A small part of his insistence that Carl come along was to show him what it was really like on assignment. Now Van Helsing realized that Carl might yet be a real asset out here.

As they got closer to the building, a female voice could be heard from inside: "My face, look what you have done to my face . . . ," the voice wept. *That's her,*

Van Helsing realized, *the vampire.* She was injured but alive—with six direct hits? It seemed impossible.

He shouldered his crossbow and continued forward. The front door suddenly blew open and Marishka raced out, backhanding Van Helsing and tossing him fifty feet through the air. His weapon flew off in a different direction as he crumpled to the ground some distance away. Carl dove out of the way as Van Helsing rolled to his feet to see the monster rip the crossbow bolts one by one from her chest and face. She soared up, then landed on a balcony, instantly transforming into a beautiful dark-haired girl with dark hair wearing white robes. Then, almost as quickly, the wounds on her chest and face healed and disappeared.

Carl leaped up and said, "This should do the trick!" The friar tossed him a steel and glass bottle that Van Helsing recognized. "Holy water!" Carl announced.

Van Helsing reached out for the bottle, but Verona dove in and snatched it. She let it drop into the well and addressed one of the others: "Finish him."

"Too bad. So sad," the one called Marishka said in a singsong voice, turning in the air toward him. Desperate, he scanned the immediate area. There had to be something he could use. . . .

Then he saw it across the square: the church and, out front, a basin of holy water. In her human form, the vampire bride was watching him closely. She looked from him to the holy water. Van Helsing prepared to move and saw that she was doing the same.

It was going to be a race, and if he was lucky, it might even be close.

Anna dashed into the first building she could find—a pub—and skidded to a halt inside. Aleera was there in human form, casually sipping a glass of suspiciously red liquid. A man lay dead across the bar next to her. Reflexively, Anna spun around to escape and saw Verona blocking her way.

Two of them—this was trouble.

"Hello, Anna, my dear," Verona said, immediately starting to move in for the kill. The princess stumbled back into a wall, realizing she was cornered.

"You won't have me, Verona" was all she could think to say.

The vampire smiled pleasantly and licked her lips. "The last of the Valerious," she remarked, revealing canine teeth horribly distended into hideous fangs.

Anna didn't hesitate: She threw a punch squarely at the creature's face. With lightning-fast agility Verona grabbed her fist. Anna felt the sheer power in the vampire's hand, which was more like an iron vise. With a squeeze and a push, Verona forced Anna to her knees.

Aleera stepped forward and shoved Verona aside. "I want first bite."

Verona grudgingly nodded her consent, and Aleera bent down for the kill.

I'm sorry Velkan, I tried, I really tried, Anna thought.

* * *

Van Helsing saw that he would never make it to the holy water before Marishka got him. However, he might be able to reach his crossbow, which was in the middle of the square, about halfway between himself and the vampire. From the railing she was perched on, Marishka raised her arms as if about to take flight and daring him to try to outmaneuver her.

Van Helsing made his move, running and diving for his weapon. Rolling to his feet, he saw that the bride of Dracula had metamorphosed back into the bat creature. It rushed over his head, creating a howling wind as he came up with his crossbow ready. Wary of the crossbow, it didn't strike and flew past him.

Van Helsing raced across the square toward the church. He could hear the creature laugh wildly from somewhere behind him. Not daring to turn around, he kept running until he reached the front of the church. Knowing that an attack could come at any moment, he moved as quickly as he could, slamming the tips of his arrows into the water. Sensing that the creature was approaching, he turned and fired in a single, fluid motion.

The bat was rocketing straight at him and was just a few yards away when the crossbow's bolts found their mark. The vampire shrieked horribly, and Van Helsing could hear the sound of sizzling flesh. Almost immediately, the creature changed direction, spiraling up into the air, then slamming into the church spire a moment later.

*   *   *

The bite of the vampire would be the last thing Anna would feel before she died, and it was seconds away now. She wished for a weapon. Even if she couldn't kill them, she wanted to hurt them—anything but to die helplessly on her knees.

Verona leaned closer, and Anna decided that if she could do nothing else, she would face her death like a Valerious, with all the dignity she could muster. Suddenly both Verona and Aleera were screaming loudly, and Anna was blown across the pub by a gale-force wind as the two brides dressed in white transformed into bats.

Van Helsing watched as two white specters crashed up through a rooftop. He tried to line them up in his sights, but they flew off, wailing insanely. A shame: He finally had a weapon that worked against these creatures.

Stepping back from the church, he could see the dying Marishka, pinned to the church spire. The crowd gathering behind him watched in silence.

The hellish bat slowly changed into an impossibly beautiful young girl, who glared down at Van Helsing and hissed. Then she began to transform once more, her flesh turning molten. Marishka looked like a living container of liquid, then began to rot and decay.

The process was quick, but her final shrieks were no less horrifying as her flesh disintegrated in front of Van Helsing. A few seconds later, the screams ceased and what was left of her body went still, slowly turning to dust.

A hush filled the square. Van Helsing scanned the crowd and found Carl nearby. Realizing the danger had passed, the villagers began to slowly crawl out from the wreckage of their town. Van Helsing allowed himself a moment of satisfaction: He had defeated one of the feared vampires—and these were creatures who could move about during the daytime as long as they avoided direct sunlight. There was hope for this village for the first time in centuries.

The people were gawking and pointing at him. There was something aggressive about the attention; it was definitely not a sign of admiration from a grateful populace.

One of them stepped forward. "He killed a bride. He killed Marishka! He killed a vampire!"

He's saying it as though it's a bad thing, Van Helsing thought. He looked over at Carl, who appeared just as confused.

The undertaker approached with an amused smile. "The vampires only kill what they need to survive, one or two people a month. Now they will kill for revenge."

Once again the villagers seemed to conjure pitchforks and weapons from nowhere and started to move in toward Carl and Van Helsing.

"Are you always this popular?" Carl asked.

"Pretty much," Van Helsing replied.

The undertaker tipped his large top hat to Van Helsing. "And what name, my good sir, do I put on *your* gravestone?" Van Helsing gripped his crossbow tighter. He hadn't wanted this fight. He had come to battle the undead, not the misguided living.

Out of nowhere, the princess appeared and stepped forward. "His name is Van Helsing."

A murmur washed over the crowd. Finally, there it was: admiration. "Van Helsing . . . It's Van Helsing . . . ," he heard. He had only been there a few hours, but already Van Helsing decided that he liked Romania better than France.

Anna gave him a nod. "Your reputation precedes you."

Van Helsing shot back a long, hard look. "Next time, stay close. You're no good to me dead."

Clearly she was not used to being spoken to with anything less than total reverence. For an instant it looked as if she might once again order them killed, but she simply laughed. "Well, I'll say this to you, you've got courage." Anna turned to the crowd. "He's the first one to kill a vampire in over a hundred years!" she proclaimed. After giving Van Helsing another appraising look, she said, "I'd say that's earned him a drink."

Dracula felt his bride die. There was her pain and her fear, and then her connection to him simply ended. Instantly alert, the count felt rage boiling inside him. Someone had destroyed what was *his*, taken something from *him* that *he* valued.

He awoke and rose, his fury melting the snow and ice that encased his coffin. *"Marishkaaa!!!"* he shouted, his voice echoing through his fortress.

He walked up the side of the enormous pillar next to his coffin. As he passed the ancient candelabra, he willed the candles to ignite. It was infuriating! A mortal, taking what was his! The living were his cattle, his food. The sheer impudence of the act astonished him.

"If it's not the Christians, it's the Moors! Why can't they just leave us alone? We never kill more than our fill. And less than our share. Can *they* say the same?"

Reaching the ice-covered ceiling, he walked across it to his two remaining brides, Verona and Aleera, who were hanging from a beam, cowering, cradled in each other's arms, and sobbing. Reaching into their minds, he took the information he needed. *The Princess. The Stranger.*

When he was face-to-face with his brides, he felt his anger rise. "Did I not say how important it was to finish with these *Valerious?* Now that we are so close to fulfilling our dream?"

The brides wailed in anguish and the count softened his tone. "There, there, my lovelies. Do not worry, I shall find another bride."

Shock and dismay registered on their faces. "Do we mean so little to you?" Aleera asked.

"Have you no heart?" Verona added.

He was immediately stern. "No! I have no heart. I feel no love. Nor fear, nor joy, nor sorrow. I am hollow! Soulless! At war with the world and every living soul in it! . . . But soon . . . very soon, the final battle will begin." Dracula smiled. "I must find out who our new visitor is." He realized that he was not completely hollow. The stranger had killed his Marishka and would pay dearly. The thought gave him some satisfaction and he licked his lips. Yes, and he collected all his debts in blood.

Jumping the forty feet to the floor, Dracula sensed another of his servants nearby. The shadow of the werewolf appeared on the wall. Turning, the count watched him pace back and forth as far as the chain around the beast's neck would allow.

The stranger would indeed know his wrath. "We'll have to make a special aperitif out of him. We are much too close to success to be interrupted now."

His brides dropped to the floor next to him. "No, my lord! Please! Say you won't try again!" Aleera pleaded.

"My heart could not bear the sorrow if we fail again," Verona added.

"Silence!" he shouted, his voice booming through the great hall. The brides cowered in fear. He regretted frightening them: They had suffered enough this day. Enveloping them in his cape, he soothed them with his voice and his will. "No, no, no. Do not fear me, you must not fear me, everyone else fears me." Verona and Aleera were soon purring in his grasp.

"But we must try . . . we have no choice but to try . . . for our own survival." Dracula inhaled, smelling his brides. Their scent was intoxicating, and for a moment he briefly could almost recall the feeling of life itself.

The spell was broken by the werewolf's howl. The count could see the beast's shadow being poked by a long stick held by a short, twisted form. Each time the stick met the werewolf's hide, there was the unmistakable sound of electric shock. "Igor!" Dracula called out.

The disfigured man scurried up to him, slipping across the ice as he carried a ten-foot cattle prod. "Yes, Master!" Igor said.

"Why do you torment that thing so?" the count asked.

"It's what I do."

"Remember, Igor: 'Do unto others . . .' "

"Yes, Master, before they do unto me," the gnarled man replied.

Dracula found he could not be angry with his servant, not when he learned his lessons so well. Besides, he needed Igor, who had now become essential to his plan. "Now go," he said, dismissing him with a wave.

Looking up into the rafters, Dracula saw his Dwergi perched along the beams. Short and squat, they looked much like the trolls of human lore. But they were very much alive, one of the few groups of mortals that Dracula found useful. Their masks and goggles made them frightening, which pleased him. They had other purposes as well, especially now.

"To Castle Frankenstein!" he called out. Yes, it was time to begin. A new age was dawning. Dracula's long wait was over.

7

VALERIOUS MANOR LOOMED OVER THE VILLAGE, DRAMATI-
cally set against the crags of the Carpathian Mountains. Clearly, the princess's family had been here for
a long time.

Van Helsing followed Anna through the house to
a large door that she pushed open, revealing the
family armory. Four centuries of lethal-looking
weaponry sat in cases and on racks: broadswords
and short swords, sabers and scimitars, as well as
maces, spears, and simple clubs. Van Helsing recognized most but not all of the weapons, and there
were some he had seen only in books.

Now *he* was impressed. Carl was looking about
wide-eyed as well, seeing that the tools around them
had been crafted by the hands of masters. Turning,
Anna inquired, "So how did you get here?"

"We came across the sea," Carl replied immediately.

Anna was uncharacteristically curious. "Really?

The sea? The Adriatic Sea?" Then she seemed to catch herself in her enthusiasm, instantly reasserting her iron control. Van Helsing could see that she wanted information from them, but she also needed to show that she was in charge, which explained why she had purposely brought them to this room to talk.

Normally he would have liked to parry with her, and he would have enjoyed the struggle for dominance, but he had a job to do, and little time in which to do it. The brides would have reported to their master by now.

"Where do I find Dracula?" he asked.

"He used to live in this very house, four centuries ago, but no one knows where he lives now," Anna replied, gesturing at a huge oil painting that covered an entire wall. It was a rich and fantastical map of Transylvania, the work of both a master artist and mapmaker. "My father would stare at that for hours, looking for Dracula's lair," she mused.

She grabbed a sword from a rack, an iron mace, and then some throwing stars. Anna was courageous, given what he had seen of the power of the vampires so far; however, even if these weapons could hurt the count or his brides, they would not kill them. "So that's why you've come: to destroy Dracula," she said.

"I can help you," he said.

"No one can help me," she replied, resignation in her voice. There it was: She was not only ready to fight but ready to lay down her life. The princess took a breath and added, "You can die trying. All of my family has. I can handle this myself."

"So I noticed," Van Helsing said.

The princess spun around, her face suffused with anger. "The vampires attacked in the daylight; they never do that. I was unprepared. It won't happen again," she declared, her tone defiant.

"Why did they attack in the daylight?" he asked, clearly wondering why the vampires would put their lives at risk.

"Clearly they wanted to catch me off guard. They seem almost desperate to finish off my family."

There was something important there; Van Helsing could feel it. "Why is that? Why now?"

"You ask a lot of questions."

Van Helsing shook his head. "Usually I ask only two: What are we dealing with? And how do I kill it?"

Anna kept moving, strapping on a metal breast-plate and two spiked gauntlets. "My father spent most of his life looking for answers, year after year." She gestured out the window at the castle tower. "Tearing apart that tower, combing through the family archives."

Van Helsing shot Carl a look. The friar was still admiring the weaponry. "The tower. Start there," he said.

"Right," Carl said, and did nothing. He merely stared at Van Helsing, as if he were waiting for something. "Now?" he finally asked.

Van Helsing's only response was a glare. "Right. The tower. *Now*," Carl said, and quickly exited.

Oblivious, Anna seized a scabbard, strapped it to

her waist, and headed for the swords. Once again, Van Helsing recognized that what she was doing was noble and brave. It also wasn't going to do them any good. He stood in her path.

"The only way to save your family is to stay alive until Dracula is killed," he said.

"And who will kill him if not me? Who will show the courage if not me?"

"If you go out there alone, you'll be outmanned and outpositioned." He pointed out the window at the growing dusk and added, "And *you* can't see in the dark."

Anna laughed him off and moved forward. Van Helsing took the opportunity to close the gap between them until he was inches from her face. There was something familiar about her eyes, a look he had seen before: Not only was she prepared to die, but she did not expect to live to see another day.

Van Helsing had two problems with this. First, half of his assignment was to protect her. Second, he needed her and what she knew to help him with the other half of his assignment: to destroy Dracula. Now that Mr. Hyde had finally been dispatched once and for all, his record was perfect: He had never failed to complete an assignment, and he didn't intend to start now.

Van Helsing stared into her eyes and said, "In the morning, we'll hunt him together."

Anna studied him before she spoke. "Some say you're a murderer, Mr. Van Helsing. Others say you're a holy man. Which is it?"

"A bit of both, I think." He felt a moment of relief; he had convinced her. It wasn't much of a victory, but it seemed like all he would get from her today.

A slight smile creased Anna's face. "I promised you a drink. The bar is down the hall. Help yourself. As for me . . ." Her face was set and the hint of humor left her eyes. "I'm going."

So much for victory. . . .

Anna grabbed a sword and slammed it into her scabbard. "I'm sorry you have to carry this burden," Van Helsing said.

"On the contrary," she said, "I would wish for it to be no other way." Van Helsing saw that she meant it. What was it that motivated her? He knew what drove him: He wanted to know who he was and reclaim his past. Also, it was simply what he did. He was good at it, and that was just enough to tide him over his long moments of doubt.

There was strength in her, but there was something else at work. Her family? Its tradition? To his surprise, Van Helsing found that he was genuinely curious about her—about things that weren't directly connected to the matter at hand, to his assignment. That was unusual for him. Of course, it would all be moot if the princess got herself killed. He watched as she grabbed a vicious-looking helmet, black metal with sharp metal flanges.

"I'm sorry about your father and brother," he said, trying to stall her. Perhaps if he got her to think about their sacrifices she would think a moment about how best to achieve the goals they died for.

110

"I *will* see them again," she replied. She saw something in his face and added, "We Transylvanians always look on the brighter side of death."

"There's a brighter side of death?"

"Yes, it's just harder to see." With that, the princess pulled her helmet on and started to charge out of the room. Van Helsing grabbed her arm, spun her around, and held one hand palm up between their faces. Then, with a single sharp breath, he blew the blue powder from his hand into her face.

The princess fell backward against a wall, out cold. Van Helsing caught her before she sank to the floor. "I'm sorry about that too."

He had kept her from going out into the night to face Dracula alone. Another small victory, but after today, Van Helsing decided that he would take what he could get.

"Listen to your brother," Mama said.

Anna stood there, mute and fuming.

"Anna," Mama said, raising her voice.

"I am ready," she replied.

"It's too dangerous," Velkan said.

"I can handle myself; even Papa says—" Anna mustered all the defiance she could.

"Papa isn't here, and until he is—" Velkan said.

"I don't have to listen to you." Anna cursed silently when she realized that her voice was too high, nearly a shriek. Then she turned and said, "Mama?"

Her mother smiled, and Anna knew she wasn't going to like what came next. "Anna, in a few years—"

"But I'm not a child." Again, Anna couldn't control the pitch of her voice.

Mama smiled again and Anna wanted to scream. "But, darling, you are a child. You're only twelve. Don't be in such a hurry."

"Velkan is only fourteen," Anna replied.

"Two years older than you," Velkan said pointedly.

"You only let him go because he's a boy," Anna said.

Mama just sighed by way of an answer. After a moment Velkan stepped forward and said gently, "Anna, Papa has new plans. If we're lucky, this will all be over before you are old enough to go. You may never have to do what we are about to do."

His soft voice, the condescending look of concern on his face. . . . Out of nowhere, tears sprang from her eyes, which horrified her. Immediately she turned away and ran for her bedroom.

It was too much. He didn't understand and neither did Mama. They wanted to protect her as if she were a helpless child, but she wasn't. She was strong, and good with a sword—almost as good as Velkan. Most of all, she wanted to help, she wanted her parents to be proud of her, and she wanted Velkan to see her for what she was: his equal.

Papa came home less than an hour later, but Anna did not go down to see him. Instead she crept to the stairs and listened while Papa, Mama, and Velkan talked in the armory. Velkan and Mama were laughing as they told Papa about their earlier argument. Papa did not join in. He only said to Mama, "She is willful, darling. She gets that from her father." The clear pride in his voice gave Anna a rush of pleasure.

112

She waited quietly for the men from the village to come and for the group to collect their weapons and leave. Afterward she raced to her room and waited for Mama, who came to bring her some tea.

"Are you all right, Anna?"

"Yes, I'm . . . sorry about before."

"It's all right. Please remember, we just want what's best for you, even Velkan," she said.

"I know, Mama." Then, thankfully, her mother left. Anna waited until she heard Mama's own bedroom door close before she moved. She would have liked to wait until Mama was asleep, but she knew that her mother would not rest until Papa and Velkan returned from the hunt.

Anna put on her riding clothes, choosing all black because it would give her the best cover in the darkness. Looking out the window, she saw the full moon hanging low in the sky. It was the first night of the harvest moon, the brightest one of the year. In other lands, she knew that the light of the harvest moon allowed farmers to work their fields late into the night. Here, that was obviously impossible, but someday it would happen again. Thanks to her family—and maybe to her—the harvest moon would once again be a symbol of life and not one of fear and death.

She crept down the stairs and slipped into the armory. The servants were all shut up in their rooms. As a rule, people moved as little as possible during full moons, which allowed Anna to move freely throughout the house.

She did not take any armor, since she didn't want anything slowing her down. Anna would have to hurry to catch up with her father. She imagined the moment when she found him. He would be angry at first, but he would have to let her remain with him for the duration of the hunt. When he saw how she carried herself, he would have to admit that she was ready. When it was over, he would be proud of her.

Anna took a sword, one of the larger sabers. It was a little heavy, but she would be damned if she let Velkan see her carrying a child's short sword. Then she grabbed some throwing stars and the most important weapon of all: a silver dagger.

Anna went to the window and opened it. Any of the doors to the outside were out of the question: There would be noise and a chance that someone would hear and try to stop her. She climbed onto the windowsill and swung her legs out, holding herself still for a moment.

She felt a pang of guilt for deceiving her family and actively disobeying her parents' wishes, but her father had said it himself: She was willful. In a little while, her family was going to find out just what she could do. Holding on to the windowsill, Anna lowered herself as far as she could, then dropped. It wasn't far, but the landing rattled her. She was outside, on her own, during a full moon! It felt wonderful! The strength of her ancestors coursed through her veins as she prepared to join the family's great battle. She knew where her father was going to begin and headed out in that direction at a trot.

Anna had gone only a few steps when she heard a howl, the sound causing a chill to run down her spine. It was the unmistakable call of a werewolf, deeper and more resonant than an ordinary wolf. The urge to stop and hide swept over her, but she forced herself to keep going, though at a careful walk now.

Anna strained to hear any sign of the hunting party or of its unearthly prey. There was nothing but the normal sounds of the night and the whistling of the wind, but they sounded like doom to her. She had the feeling that she was being watched from all sides. The only comfort she had was that if a werewolf had seen her, it wouldn't have waited to pounce.

For half an hour, Anna trudged through the fields and scattered trees until she reached the woods. She was tempted to call out for her father, a move that would be not only foolish but suicidal.

What if I can't find them?

One of the first rules of the hunt was that no one ever went out alone. Werewolves were much more likely to pick off people on their own . . . as she was. A twig snapped somewhere to her left, and her head spun in that direction. There was a sound like footfalls. Her heart began to pound, and she told herself that it must be the rustling of the wind on the leaves.

The wind . . .

She remembered that the wind was important. It carried scents, and the sense of smell was one of the werewolves' keenest. Anna had to stay upwind of the beast so it didn't catch her scent, but how could she do that if she didn't know where it was?

As for herself, Anna could smell only the slightly damp fallen leaves. The forest was dead silent: there were no small animals scurrying about, not even the song of crickets in the night. There could be only one reason for this: a dark force at work, a predator afoot that all the other creatures feared.

Suddenly, Anna wanted her room and the comfort of her warm bed, and considered heading back home. If she was lucky, she could slip back into the house and no one would ever know she had been gone. But pride kept her from going back; instead she followed the path that ran at the foot of the mountains. Her father had shown it to her before in the safety of daylight.

Fear kept Anna's senses sharp as she remained on the lookout for any sign of danger. Then she definitely heard the sound of footfalls. *That's him, that's Papa,* she thought.

The sounds of movement came closer. She approached a clearing in the trees and stopped, not wishing to step out into the open until she was sure it was her father's hunting party and not their quarry.

Then silence, except for the breeze through the trees. Perhaps it had just been her imagination. Enough was enough: She would go back home. Next time, she would just convince Papa to let her come with him.

Anna turned to head for Valerious Manor . . . and then for the first time in her life saw a werewolf in the flesh. The monster loomed above her, blocking her path. It was more than seven feet tall, powerfully muscled, and standing on its hind legs like a man, its breath blowing white vapor in the cool moonlit night. The creature's face was more wolf than human, with large pointed ears and a pronounced snout with large canine teeth. The only quality that distinguished it from the face of an animal was the terrible intelligence in its eyes. Standing less than ten yards away, the creature was utterly still and silent, watching her.

Anna's heart seemed to stop, then thunder in her chest.

The werewolf looked down at her, and she had seconds before it struck. Raising its head, it gave a howl so loud and deep that she could feel it resonating in her chest.

Suddenly, Anna grabbed the silver dagger at her side and leaped to her feet. Before a plan had even formed in her mind, she was hurling herself at the beast, even as she felt something strike her hard on one side. She was airborne again and then she felt nothing. . . .

Seconds or minutes or hours later, Anna opened her eyes. As she tried to clear her head, she realized she was on her back and being dragged forward. But that was impossible, because she had to be . . . dead.

Anna willed her blurred vision to clear. Hazily she saw the back of the werewolf walking in front of her—its large clawed hand clutched her boot-encased foot, and the beast was dragging her along like a dead rabbit.

Somehow she was still alive. The creature pulled her into a clearing, where she saw another werewolf waiting. This one was smaller, perhaps an adolescent.

In an instant, Anna understood. The adult werewolf hadn't spared her; it had carried her off to feed its young. She tried to pull her foot out of the creature's iron grasp. It held her firmly as she struggled and screamed. "Papa!" she cried over and over. "Help me, Papa!"

The werewolf paid no attention. It grabbed her with both hands, tossing her in front of the younger creature, who let out a howl of its own. Dazed from the fall, Anna was too frightened to even scream. She waited for it to pounce and saw a flash of movement, but it wasn't the creature. Something small flew across her field of vision and into the chest of the young werewolf.

Anna saw the Valerious family crest on the hilt of the weapon buried in the creature's breast. It was her brother's silver dagger!

"Anna, run!" Velkan's voice boomed. She could do nothing but watch the young monster double over and loudly whimper. Velkan had hit it directly in the heart.

It fell at Anna's feet, dead.

The elder werewolf screamed in rage and whirled on Velkan, whom she could now see standing at the edge of the clearing. Her brother had his sword out in front of him, an open challenge to the creature.

He was alone.

"Run, Anna!" he shouted.

This was all wrong. Where was Papa? Where were the others? They must have split up to look for her. Papa had the revolver with the silver bullets, otherwise Velkan would have used it already.

The werewolf attacked, swinging at Velkan, who struck out with the sword, catching the monster on the arm and rolling under it. As it howled in pain, Velkan jumped to his feet.

The creature struck again and Velkan parried with the sword, connecting with the beast's other arm. The werewolf bellowed again. This couldn't last long: Velkan could injure the werewolf with his blade, but without silver he could not kill it.

Her brother seemed to realize the same thing and yelled out again, "Anna, run, get out of here!"

No, *she thought.* If I go, Velkan will be left alone, and then it will just be a matter of time. I may be a child, but I'm not completely helpless, and that's my brother out there.

Anna was on her feet, reaching for the pocket that held her throwing stars. Velkan was knocked on his back, sword out, the monster above him.

There was no more time to think. She grabbed the stars with her left hand, and one by one she passed them to her right and let them fly.

One . . . two . . . three . . . four . . . five . . . six.

The werewolf screamed in pain and turned to face her. Velkan jumped up and thrust forward with his sword. The blade went into the creature's back and came out in front. It roared, clawing at the weapon, which had been wrenched out of Velkan's grasp.

The monster spun around in a circle, pulling at the sword from both front and back. It didn't budge. Anna felt a twinge of hope. Velkan had hurt it—badly.

But it was not enough. They couldn't kill it with a hundred steel swords. They needed silver . . . a silver dagger.

Anna searched the clearing for the other werewolf. For a crazy moment, she thought it had disappeared, until she saw that it had transformed: The monster was gone, and in its place was a boy of perhaps thirteen, her brother's knife sticking out of his chest.

He's just a little older than I am, *she thought. Then she pushed the thought aside. Running to the boy, she pulled out the dagger. The older werewolf had given up trying to extract the sword. Unsteady on its feet, the monster was eyeing Velkan.*

The werewolf began to close in on her brother. Could she hit it with the dagger from where she was? No, it was too far. To kill it instantly, she would have to aim directly for the heart; otherwise it would live long enough to kill or bite her brother . . . and the bite was worse than a death sentence.

"Velkan!" Anna called out, and threw the knife to him. It sailed end over end toward her brother, who held out his hand.

If he misses . . . , she thought.

But Velkan caught it. He drew his arm back and threw it without hesitating.

The dagger caught the werewolf in the center of its chest. It barely had time to clutch at the knife before it fell over in a dead heap. Anna watched in horrified fascination as the beast shrank into the form of a man of about Papa's age. It shed the skin of the wolf, revealing the person underneath. A moment later the hide of the creature disappeared, leaving only the man.

Velkan was in front of her, grasping her by the shoulders, concern on his face. "Are you hurt? Did it hurt you? Did it bite you?"

Anna took a quick inventory of herself: scrapes and bruises but no cuts, and more importantly, no bites. "No, I'm . . . okay."

Her brother took that in and Anna waited for what would come next: the shouts, the recriminations. She deserved them all. But as she watched her sibling's face, he did something that shocked her more than anything else had in her young life: Velkan burst into tears. His face just collapsed as he hugged her tightly and fell to his knees, still clutching her to him. "I thought we'd lost you . . . ," he said between sobs.

Anna hugged her brother back, her own tears mixing with his. In her mind, she begged his forgiveness and

121

promised herself and God that she would never let Velkan or the rest of her family down again.

Velkan . . . , Anna thought as she woke up. He was alive! She had just seen him!

No, it was a dream. Though she had visions of her brother every night since his death, this was the one she had most often.

That made sense. It was the first time she had failed her family and her brother. The second time was a month ago, when Velkan paid with his life. Hot grief ran through her body. Like every morning for the month—the last cycle of the moon—she felt her brother die again.

Anna shook herself awake. Something was wrong. It was still dark and she shouldn't be here; she should be out there fighting.

Van Helsing! He had done this to her: drugged her and put her to sleep so that she would not go out alone. He was impossible. *He had no right!*

To what? To save your life? To keep you from making the same mistake you made when you were twelve? a voice in her head demanded.

No, he had no right to interfere! She was still wearing her clothes, though her armor and weapons had been removed. She cursed under her breath and quickly sat up.

Pain shot through her skull, and her hand went to her head. "Oh my God, that hurts. . . . That son of a bitch." Ignoring her screaming headache, she leaped out of bed and stormed for the door.

Once in the hallway, she realized that the house was deathly quiet—not unusual for a full moon, but after the action-charged day, Anna found herself exceptionally alert. She was pleased to feel the grogginess from the drug Van Helsing had blown into her face begin to lift. The light from the lanterns hanging on the wall was dim, but enough for her to see for several yards in any direction.

She pricked up her ears, but heard nothing except for the rain against the windows. There was a creak, normal for the family house, given its age. Reaching up, she took a lantern off the wall.

A minute or so later she was in the armory, the place where she felt safest. Another creak. Suddenly she knew that someone else was nearby. In that moment, she felt like a twelve-year-old girl again.

"Van Helsing?" Anna called loudly.

Another noise came from somewhere near the cases that held her family's arms. She scanned the gloom of the armory. Cocking her arm holding the lantern, she prepared to strike at whoever or whatever it was. She moved toward the source of the sound and slowly peeked around a corner.

A window had been left open, and the wind and rain were knocking the shutters against the wall. Cursing herself for being such a fool, Anna breathed a sigh of relief and pulled the window closed, her eyes fixing on the full moon hanging outside. As she turned away, she saw the wet paw prints on the floor.

Her breath caught in her throat, but she forced

her eyes to follow the prints to the center of the room . . . where they stopped. One of them was in here, with her.

Setting her lantern down, Anna grabbed a morningstar from its mount. She could sense its presence. Her instincts were screaming, but she had no idea where the creature was. Readying herself, she weaved through the cases of her family's deadly weaponry.

Anna was no longer a frightened twelve-year-old girl; she was a grown woman who had seen her share of fighting and death. If there was a werewolf in her family's house, she was prepared to give it the last surprise of its unholy life.

A long, low growl resonated through the room. Anna froze in the middle of the armory and drew her arm back, ready to strike a blow.

A single drop of rain fell onto her cheek. Anna instantly looked up and had no trouble making out the werewolf among the shadows. It was dangling from a beam above her, its eyes staring down.

The creature roared, and Anna ran for the door. Turning the corner of one of the weapon cases, she felt her body slam into something.

The werewolf, her mind supplied. Anna screamed and started to swing the weapon, but the creature grabbed her hands. . . . No, not the creature: a man. Velkan! She was too stunned to speak or move. Relief and then joy flooded through her, and the month of grief and of missing her brother briefly disappeared. In that moment even the werewolf in the room was forgotten.

"Velkan! Oh my God! You're alive!"

"Quiet, Anna, I only have a moment."

Then she remembered: "But, Velkan, there's a werewolf!"

His face was deadly serious. "Never mind that! Listen to me! I know Dracula's secrets! He has . . ." Velkan hesitated and said, ". . . mumblich . . . Nowger . . . lochen . . ."

A struggle played out on his face. Velkan was hurt. He couldn't seem to control his mouth, and his clothes were torn nearly to shreds. Then Velkan started to spasm and jerk as if losing control of much more than his mouth. Suddenly he lurched to the wall and *climbed it.*

Anna's mind protested: *No, the werewolf is up there . . . !*

A terrible realization began to dawn on her.

She saw Velkan turn his head to the window, where the full moon appeared from behind the cloud cover.

"Anna! *Run!*" he shouted.

No! He was her brother, he needed help, no matter what was happening to him! Before her eyes, Velkan began to change. His body seemed to relax, then increase in size. For a second, it looked as if there were something inside him too large for his skin, which began to bulge and move in odd ways . . . ripping and shredding until the werewolf underneath emerged. This was not her brother . . . it couldn't be. . . .

The door burst open, and Van Helsing raced in with his guns drawn.

Anna turned back to see the werewolf throw itself through the door to the balcony, raining glass and water into the armory as Van Helsing ran up to her.

"Are you all right?"

Before she could respond, Van Helsing was already at the balcony and looking outside for the creature . . . for Velkan.

Van Helsing watched as the creature climbed horizontally across the side of the manor house. After a few steps, it vaulted off, splashing down into the river and heading into the village. There was a noise from inside, and Van Helsing spun around to see Carl entering the armory.

Sniffing the air, the friar said, "Why does it smell like wet dog in here?"

Van Helsing holstered his revolvers and headed for the door. "Werewolf."

"Ah! Right. You'll be needing silver bullets, then," Carl replied. He began to scrounge around in his frock and pulled out a bandolier filled with gleaming ammunition. He tossed it to Van Helsing, who pulled it from the air and slung it over his shoulder.

By then Anna had sufficiently recovered from the state of shock she had been in. "No. Wait!"

There was no time. She would want to come along, but she was safer in the house. Exiting the armory at a run, Van Helsing slammed the door behind him. The pounding coming from inside made him think that if she was upset at him for the knockout powder, she was going to be even more furious now.

"Van Helsing!" she was shouting. He shut her out and concentrated on the task ahead, dashing outside into the stormy night. The hunt had begun.

He made for the village on foot. The streets were a labyrinth of shops and homes; the only sounds were the muffled revelry coming from the many pubs. It was remarkable: just a few hours earlier vampires attacked the village, and now people were living it up. A strange town indeed! Van Helsing wondered how much they had seen over the years.

He soon reached the state of heightened concentration that he felt only when he was hunting one of the dark creatures: entirely aware of every sound, every smell, every movement in his field of vision.

Anna's expression before he left her appeared in his mind. There had been something wrong with it. There was fear, but there was also . . . something else. And how had she survived for that long in the same room with a werewolf?

A smell. His prey was near; the odor was strong. "Wet dog," he said out loud.

A flash of fur exploded out of a distant alley, and there was a blur of incredible speed as the werewolf weaved back and forth across the street, from doorway to doorway, getting closer and closer. Van Helsing brought his guns to bear, but somehow the creature always managed to stay one step ahead of his aim.

In a single bound, it vanished into an alley twenty feet in front of him. The game had changed. A sense older and deeper than the five common ones told

Van Helsing what it was. He took a few steps backward and said to himself, "Who's hunting who?"

The werewolf was tracking him, he was sure of it, and narrow alleys were not a good place for him to face the monster. Van Helsing kept moving until he found what he was looking for: the open area of Vaseria's graveyard.

There was a sound nearby. Van Helsing spun around a corner and slammed his back up against the wall, preparing himself for the attack that would come at any moment. Nothing. Quiet again—too much for his liking. Something smashed against the wall next to him. Whipping his gun around, Van Helsing pointed it at the figure by his side. In the moonlight, the cadaverous face of the undertaker looked much more like a skull than flesh and blood.

Van Helsing saw what had hit the wall next to him: a coffin. The undertaker smiled down the barrels of Van Helsing's pistols, a smile as odd and joyless as his eyes. Somehow he fit well in this strange place. As Van Helsing lowered his guns, the undertaker tipped his hat, gestured at the coffin, and said, "Well, look at this, a perfect fit. What a coincidence." He headed into the graveyard carrying a shovel. "I see the Wolf Man hasn't killed you."

"Don't worry, he's getting to it," Van Helsing replied, raising his guns again. He headed into the cemetery behind the undertaker.

"You don't seem too worried about him," Van Helsing continued.

"Oh, I'm no threat to him, and I'm the one who

cleans up after him. If you get my meaning." Van Helsing noted that this was a man who enjoyed his work entirely too much.

The undertaker broke the earth with his shovel and commenced digging a fresh grave. How much business had Dracula's minions given this man? And how long had the count and the undertaker been in their odd, unspoken partnership?

"Little late to be digging graves, isn't it?" Van Helsing asked.

"Never too late to dig graves. Never know when you'll need a fresh one."

A sound from behind him. Van Helsing whirled, his eyes scanning the darkness.

Danger! his mind screamed, and he spun around just in time: The undertaker was swinging the heavy shovel at Van Helsing's head. Moving as if with a mind of its own, Van Helsing's hand caught it when it was inches from smashing into his face. Suddenly he wondered how "unspoken" the man's partnership with Dracula really was.

Now the undertaker looked terrified. He saw the undertaker's glance shift slightly to one side to look briefly over Van Helsing's shoulder. That was all the warning needed.

A massive blur flew out of the darkness behind him. The werewolf hit the undertaker head-on, sending his top hat flying. Together, man and beast shot sixty feet down the alley. The undertaker was dead even before the two of them struck the lamppost. Dazed, the werewolf staggered to its feet. Van

Helsing's guns were already in his hands, the creature in his sights.

"No!" someone shouted as hands hit his pistols, knocking them upward so that they fired into the sky.

The werewolf disappeared around a corner. Van Helsing charged after it, only to see it dart into the dark forest. Anna ran up behind him, and Van Helsing furiously grabbed her by the throat, pinning her to the nearest wall.

"*Why?!*" he shouted. His grip was so tight that she couldn't breathe.

"You're . . . you're choking me," she sputtered.

"Give me a reason not to," Van Helsing said through clenched teeth.

Anna stared wild-eyed at him, frightened, but he could see that she wasn't about to tell him anything. He loosened his grip slightly.

"I can't. . . . if people knew . . . ," she said.

Van Helsing studied her face and then let her go. As she struggled for breath, he felt the anger draining out of him. "He's not your brother anymore, Anna."

"You knew?"

"I guessed," he said.

"*Before* or *after* I stopped you from shooting him?"

He knew she wouldn't be happy with the answer. "Before," he said.

Now it was her turn to be livid. "And still you tried to kill him?"

"He's a werewolf! He's going to kill people," Van

Helsing said, but he saw she already knew that better than anyone.

"He can't help it. It's not his fault."

"I know, but he'll do it anyway," he said.

She studied him for a minute. "Do you understand forgiveness?"

"I ask for it often," Van Helsing replied.

Resolve set on her face. "They say Dracula has a cure. If there's a chance I can save my brother, I'm going after it." Anna started to storm off, but his hand shot out and grabbed her.

"I need to find Dracula," Van Helsing said. *And to do it I need you, preferably alive*, he added to himself.

The resolve on her face faltered, and tears welled up in her eyes. Gone was the princess, the strong woman, the tough slayer of monsters. Now she looked like a girl, heartbroken and desperate to save her sibling. "I despise Dracula more than you can ever imagine. He has taken everything from me, leaving me alone in the world." She slumped back against the wall, drained. Seeing her grief, Van Helsing realized that there was something worse than having no past.

"To have memories of those you loved and lost is perhaps harder than to have no memories at all," he said, sighing. To help her was foolish and dangerous. It would distract him from his assignment; it might even help Dracula, and it would definitely make the cardinal furious. . . so at least it had a positive aspect.

Van Helsing smiled to himself and said, "All right, Anna, let's look for your brother."

8

DRACULA WATCHED THE DWERGI AT WORK. THEY WERE DIS-
gusting creatures, even by his standards, but even the
living could have their uses. Victor Frankenstein had
certainly been useful. He had built this laboratory,
something that no other living man could have
done—and the count had to acknowledge that he
himself could not have, either. That admission was not
easy for him; even in life he had been an exceptional
man: a soldier, a statesman, an alchemist, working at
the height of his time's scientific knowledge.

Now, in death, he was much more than that, and
even Frankenstein's great genius had bent easily
enough to Dracula's will.

His minions looked at him expectantly and he
nodded his approval. A Dwerger's small gloved
hand slammed a huge switch down, and the laboratory sparked to life. Brilliant arcs of electricity shot
up and down the walls as the massive dynamos,

generators, and machinery hummed and churned. The Dwergi scurried around, feverishly preparing the equipment.

There was a flash of lightning, and Dracula looked up at the shattered skylight, which he had smashed when he flew out of the lab on the night of Frankenstein's successful experiment. "Igor!" he shouted.

The twisted little man looked down from the skylight, the heavy wind practically blowing him off his feet. The count had been right to place him in Frankenstein's employ. Igor had been able to help repair the broken equipment and had helped him figure out how to operate the machinery. He was also naturally cruel and deceitful, traits that Dracula appreciated.

"Yes, Master!" Igor called down.

"Have you finished?" he asked.

"Yes, all is done! We're coming down to make the final attachments!"

"Good." Yes, the living had their uses . . . even the ones that did not serve as food.

Dracula sensed another of his servants nearby. The werewolf glided in through a fissure in the granite wall, its eyes on Dracula. The creature was still struggling under Dracula's control. Well, that would not last long. He purposely ignored the beast. "Werewolves are such a nuisance during their first full moon. So hard to control."

The gathering storm clouds and absence of moonlight quickly took effect—the creature began to shrink and shed its fur. A few moments later, the great Prince Velkan of the house of Valerious lay bent over in agony before him.

Dracula stepped around him. "I send you on a simple errand, to find out who our new friend is, and you stop for a talk with your sister." He had witnessed that exchange in his mind and found it troubling. Though Velkan had not revealed anything critical, when the moon was hidden behind clouds he had been able to effect a temporary transformation back to his human form.

"Leave her out of this, Count!" Velkan spat out. "She doesn't know your secret, and I am soon to take it to my grave."

Yes, he is strong, indeed, to defy me in thought even now. Dracula would enjoy this. He stepped up to the filthy iron pod that had once brought life to Frankenstein's creature. The new occupant of the pod had not been so lucky—inside the device was a badly burned corpse.

"Don't wish for death so quickly. I intend for you to be quite useful," Dracula offered, relishing the thought of what he was about to do to Velkan.

"I would rather die than help you," Velkan said.

"Don't be boring. Everyone who says that dies," the count replied. It had certainly been true for Victor Frankenstein. Dracula unfastened the metal straps that held the corpse. "Besides, tonight, after the final stroke of midnight, you'll have no choice but to obey me."

Dracula used one hand to rip the blackened body

from the pod and throw it in front of Velkan. "Look familiar?" he asked with anticipation.

Velkan took in the seared form and there was a flash of recognition in his eyes. "Father," he whispered. Pain crossed the prince's face as he realized that all the time his father had been missing, he had been in Dracula's grasp. The count could see Velkan imagining what horrors had been inflicted on his greatest enemy: Lord Valerious himself.

Dracula's treatment of his nemesis had been harsh. In the end, Valerious had been too weak to survive. However, even in death, he had proven beneficial. Dracula had repeated Frankenstein's experiment on Lord Valerious's corpse—unsuccessfully of course, but the attempt led Dracula to some new adjustments in the scientific experiment.

The count would have liked to savor the moment of torture on Velkan's face longer, but he had more important business. Grabbing the prince, Dracula lifted him off his feet and slammed him into the pod.

Igor barked orders at several of the Dwergi and they quickly strapped Velkan tight.

"He proved useless. But I'm hoping that with werewolf venom running through your veins, you will be of greater benefit." The count banged the rusty metal skullcap onto Velkan's head, attaching the cap's wires and electrodes to the dynamos. Already recovered from his last transformation, Velkan struggled against the bonds that held him. In truth, it was a reasonably good display of human strength and effort. Of course, it was pointless.

"I may have failed to kill you, Count, but my sister will not," he vowed, his voice rising in defiance as he continued to struggle against the restraints.

With Anna beside him on her horse, Van Helsing trotted his own mount down the snowy country lane. His eyes scanned the forest and the road. He noted with interest that Anna was looking around in the same way. Even now, when she was consumed with thoughts of her brother, she was behaving as if she were on the hunt for the battle with the darkest forces in this world and the next.

"For me, this is all personal: It's about family and honor," she said. Van Helsing understood, at least intellectually. He had no family that he could remember. The princess peered at him, curious. "Why do *you* do it?" she asked. "This *job* of yours: What do you hope to get out of it?"

"I don't know . . . maybe some self-realization," he said, but his reasons now felt small compared to hers.

"What have you gotten out of it so far?" she asked, almost as if she were sensing his thoughts.

"Back pains," he said, a trace of humor creeping into his voice. Anna smiled, and Van Helsing found himself returning it. The moment was broken when they both spotted something ahead on the road. Simultaneously they sprang from their horses. Anna reached it first and held up a long, coarse hair.

"Werewolves only shed before their first full moon. Before the curse has completely consumed them," she said.

136

Lightning flashed, and seconds later there was a clap of thunder. Van Helsing looked into the distance where a castle loomed over the countryside. More lightning momentarily illuminated the structure. There were also spectacular arcs of electricity coming from within. Something strange was going on in there, and whatever it was, Van Helsing was certain he knew who was behind it.

Without a word, he and Anna rode for the castle. Minutes later, they reached a decrepit old barn next to the main building. As they dismounted, Anna said, "I don't understand. The man who lived here was killed a year ago, along with a hideous creature he created."

"That's when your father went missing," Van Helsing said.

"Just after that."

Van Helsing debated telling her more, but what could he really say? That his instincts told him Dracula was here? Instead, they simply strapped their horses to a post.

Stepping across the snow and up to the edge of the barn, they stared past the battered front gate to the castle, where electricity flashed in a window high up in the main tower. That display seemed to be all the explanation the princess needed.

"Vampires, werewolves, lightning in winter . . . this truly is a nightmarish place," Van Helsing remarked.

Anna just stared at the hideous-looking castle, lost in her own thoughts. "I've never been to the

She felt a scream building in her throat but held it down. She had to remain calm: There was something she had to do. . . .

The sword.

Slowly she reached for it with her right hand. The were-wolf watched her with interest but didn't move. Feeling the hilt of the weapon with her fingers, Anna knew she would have only one chance at this. If she didn't strike the wolf hard and fast, she would never get close enough to use the dagger.

Pulling up on the sword, Anna felt it catch in the scabbard. Panic began to well up inside her and Anna fought it. Then she realized that the tip of the scabbard had gotten stuck in the ground. She cursed her pride, which had not allowed her to bring a shorter sword that she could draw easily. Angling the weapon backward, she was able to slowly draw it.

The quiet was broken by the werewolf's growl, and Anna simultaneously did two things: she shrieked and let go of the sword. When the creature took a step toward her, Anna instinctively ran for her life. Something hit her and she flew forward into the clearing. The werewolf had struck her from behind. She twisted around to see it looming over her from just a few feet away.

I'm finished. *Fear mixed with humiliation filled her. Mama and Velkan were right: She was just a silly girl who would die this night, and her parents would probably never even know what had happened to her. Her last act would be to bring shame to the family Valerious.*

Will he kill me immediately? *she wondered.* Or will he play with me for a while before he eats me?

117

escape hatch. They would have missed it entirely had it not been hanging at an odd angle due to a broken hinge. Once inside, their boots quietly splashing through the dirty water that covered the floor, they found themselves in the middle of a large foyer that had seen better days. The place smelled of death and corruption. Dracula was here; Van Helsing could feel it. At the far end of the hall, a small figure scurried past. Van Helsing shouldered his shotgun. Anna nodded and said, "Dwerger."

"Dwerger?" he asked.

"One of Dracula's servants. If you get the chance to kill one, do it, because they'd do worse to you."

"Right."

Another mysterious Dwerger stepped into view. Van Helsing saw it was wearing rags and some sort of mask and goggles. Van Helsing lowered the shotgun.

The Dwerger screeched at something up above him. Anna turned to Van Helsing, stricken. "They're using my brother for some sort of experiment."

"Anna," was all he could say.

She was desperate. "My brother is still battling the sickness within him. There's still hope."

He grabbed her arm and kept his voice low. "Anna! There is no hope for your brother, but we can still protect others by killing Dracula." It hurt him to say it—and he knew it hurt her to hear it—but it was true. They could still accomplish something here, something important that would give her brother's death—and all of her family's sacrifices—lasting meaning.

In her eyes, he saw the beginning of that understanding. Van Helsing could only stare back at her, the apology written on his face.

Lightning filled the sky, and Dracula smiled. It was another servant of his will. He commanded the storm the way he controlled the werewolves, using the cursed creatures to do his bidding.

The Dwergi scurried about, tending to the equipment. The balance of forces was delicate in Frankenstein's work: the slightest miscalculation and the test subject would be rendered useless—much like the late and charred Lord Valerious.

The count had been frustrated to find that some of Frankenstein's notes were missing, as were his journals—an unpleasant surprise, but one that he had been able to compensate for. The werewolf venom made Velkan stronger, less susceptible to subtle variations in the process.

Electrical power crackled. The dynamos and generators whirled. The chemical reaction tank bubbled. Everything started to accelerate. Yes, the time was near.

The count turned a flywheel, and the pod holding Velkan rose up off the floor, heading for the skylight high above.

Van Helsing and Anna came around a huge stone column and stared at the odd sight that awaited them: Hanging from the rafters, the ceiling, and various beams were dozens of gooey white maggotlike cocoons. Slime dripped to the floor as a putrid stench filled their nostrils.

"You ever see these before?" Van Helsing asked.

Anna shook her head, clearly as revolted as he was. "What do you think they are?"

Van Helsing stepped up to the closest one. The realization was instantaneous. "Offspring."

"What?" she asked.

"A man living with three gorgeous women for four hundred years?" He cocked his eyebrow and waited for that to sink in. She looked out over the cocoons.

"Vampires are the walking dead; it only makes sense that their children are born dead," she said.

Wires stuck out from all the cocoons. "He must be trying to find a way to bring them to life." Van Helsing was chilled to the bone at the prospect. He followed the wires with his eyes as they twisted together and wended their way up the massive stairs into the flickering room far above. "I was told Dracula and his brides only killed one or two people a month."

He opened his shotgun with one hand and smashed open a box of shells with the other. This was special ammunition, designed by Carl and made largely from silver nitrate.

"If they bring all of these things to life . . ." Van Helsing did not have to finish. Instead, he started pumping the special shells into his weapon.

* * *

Dracula stepped up to the chemical-reaction tank, slamming the iron hatch down and securing it. "Let us begin!" he declared.

Igor and the Dwergi clambered up the scaffolding that hung over the lab to their various stations. The storm was growing in power. Gusts of rain whipped down from the shattered skylight. Bright flashes of lightning split the night, followed by loud explosions of thunder. It was the beginning of a new age on earth, and it was exhilarating.

A bolt of electricity struck the conductor above the pod. The count could imagine it coursing through Velkan's body. It would be very painful, and the thought pleased him. An instant later, the surge of energy coursed through the wires, momentarily banishing all the shadows in the laboratory.

For Dracula, it almost felt like being alive.

Van Helsing reached for one of the cocoons. Its shell was soft, and he was able to force his fingers inside, even as his stomach twisted in protest. It was revolting work, *the work of a trash collector,* he thought wryly. The foul smell worsened as he felt the thick, cold slime.

A startling flash and a boom shook the room, and the electrical wires in front of them began to jump like scalded snakes. Van Helsing fought the impulse to pull his hand out. Instead he kept digging, steeling himself for what he would find.

There it was: something solid inside the viscous mass.

Making the hole larger, he could finally see it from the outside: the small almost human-looking face of a bat creature.

It looked like the monsters he had faced earlier that day, but rounder and stockier. Its eyes were large, dark, and lidless. A hairy pig snout sat over a gaping mouth filled with rows of tiny, razor-sharp teeth that were mottled and green.

Despite the fact that the infant monster's eyes were open, it was completely lifeless. Van Helsing felt his own stomach twisting again as he gazed at the unnatural form. Looking at Anna, Van Helsing could see that she was also sickened at the sight of it.

Another flash and boom, and the wires all around crackled with energy. The disgusting little creature snapped to life in front of them, hissing. Anna screamed reflexively. Van Helsing clamped his hand over her mouth—deliberately not using the one that had just been rooting in the cocoon's filth. Pulling the princess tightly to him, he watched as all of the sacs began pulsing with life.

Then there was a sound above them, and Van Helsing saw the two remaining brides and a man dressed all in black stride out of the flickering electrical light of the laboratory onto a balcony. *Dracula.* The vampires did not notice them. He and Anna started backing off into the darkness as a third flash of energy ripped down all the electrical wires. The cocoons began to quiver wildly. The pygmy bat creature that Van Helsing had been prodding exploded out of its cocoon, darting up into the rafters on

143

wings that were several feet across. More cocoons burst open, spraying the walls and pillars with white slime.

The newborn monsters were flying around in the foyer, their hissing and chittering becoming deafening.

Dracula's voice boomed from above: "They must feed. Show them how. And beg the Devil that this time they stay alive!"

The two brides took flight with their offspring, and Van Helsing felt a chill at the thought of what they would all do to the people in the countryside. Dracula's voice bellowed, "You must feed! To the village! *To the village!*"

"This is where I come in," Van Helsing said. He whirled into the foyer, glad to see that it was now clear of the creatures, which had all flown up higher to be with their parents.

"No! Wait! You can't!" Anna called out.

Van Helsing cocked his shotgun just as all the windows in the foyer shattered and the brides and the bat creatures started to fly out. He opened fire, pumping controlled bursts of silver nitrate that flashed through the air. The blasts hit several of the hideous things and they exploded into black goo.

As he continued to fire, Van Helsing spared a glance upward and saw Dracula watching him, insanely furious. He slammed his shotgun into the holster strapped across his back. "Now that I have your attention . . ."

A moment later, Van Helsing wondered if attracting the attention of the count was wise when Dracula screamed in rage and leaped off the eighty-foot-high balcony, diving straight for him. Van Helsing and Anna scrambled to escape. From somewhere above them they heard the pounding of large wings and felt strong gusts of wind: Dracula had transformed into a bat creature himself.

The turbulence threw around small objects and large, almost knocking Anna off her feet as she bolted out from behind a stone column and raced up the staircase—toward the laboratory and her brother. Van Helsing suppressed the urge to follow her. The count was after him now, and she would be safest wherever he wasn't. . . .

As suddenly as it had begun, the wind subsided. Van Helsing kept moving, even as he heard Dracula's voice: "I can tell the character of a man by the sound of his heartbeat. Usually when I approach I can almost dance to the beat. . . . Strange that yours is so steady."

If Dracula could hear his heartbeat, it wouldn't matter how fast or how far he went; the count would find him. Van Helsing ran anyway.

Carl thought he could happily stay in the Valerious tower bedroom for years. There were books he had not seen even in the Vatican's well-stocked libraries. Folklore, history, spirituality, as well as science and mathematics . . . relics and ancient artifacts that he could not even identify.

Almost hating to spoil the order of the collection, he had done his best to arrange the materials he needed as carefully as he could around the large canopy bed that temporarily served as his desk. He was reading a Latin text that he would have to tell the cardinal about: a sacred book written by a second-century priest whom he had never heard of, full of case studies of exorcisms and the earliest incarnations of the rites of the Church. It was also one of the most remarkable books he had ever read.

"Well, that's interesting . . . ," he thought out loud.

His concentration was broken by a horrible chittering from outside. Running to a window, he looked out and saw what appeared to be flying monkeys soaring over the dark countryside.

Whatever they were, they were about to inflict some serious harm. Without hesitating another second, Carl ran out of the room. He made his way down the stairs and shouted for the servants to stay inside. As he exited the house, he noted that he really should be following his own advice. Well, it couldn't be helped; he had to warn the villagers.

Racing for the town, he got there just ahead of the creatures. Dozens of people were standing in the town square, and several men and an attractive barmaid came out of a pub to join them—all staring up at the coming storm.

Looking over his shoulder, he saw that the swarm was very close, with the two brides leading the charge in their own bat forms. The resemblance was unmistakable, and Carl suddenly understood what the smaller creatures were.

"Oh my God! What do we do? What do we do?" he heard the barmaid ask.

To Carl it was obvious: He ran up to her, yelling, "RUN!"

He yanked the woman into a doorway as the hideous bats descended on the square. The crowd scattered. Carl saw the monsters snatch people up and carry them into the air or join together to maul unlucky villagers.

The creatures were powerful, and there were so many of them! *God help us,* Carl thought as the barmaid clutched him tightly.

9

ANNA KEPT HER HAND ON THE HILT OF THE SABER AS SHE crept up the stairs. Dracula had gone after Van Helsing, and his brides had left with their undead young. That meant that whatever servants the count had left behind were mortal . . . and vulnerable.

At the top of the stairs, the princess drew her sword. The laboratory was large and full of machinery, some of which she recognized but most of which she did not. Electricity arced and twisted, flashing all around amid a loud mix of sounds. Those terrible Dwergi were racing about, and a small deformed man with a twisted back was shouting over the noise. She had heard of this man, Igor, and knew that he had been working for Dr. Frankenstein. There had been a scandal involving grave robbing, and Igor had disappeared the night Frankenstein and his monster were killed.

"We're losing power! The human is insufficient!

Accelerate the generators! Power the dynamos!" Igor ordered.

Looking up, Anna saw the pod high above the skylight. *Velkan is in there*, she thought in horror. A bolt of lightning struck it and Anna winced as one of her brother's arms started flailing wildly. He was alive! But werewolf blood or no, he couldn't last long under the constant assault of the lightning. "Velkan," she said, climbing a nearby ladder.

It ended on a catwalk that ringed the tower twenty feet below the roof. Stepping onto it, Anna headed toward the next ladder, leading the way with her sword. At the halfway point she heard a scream from the Dwergi. She glanced either way: There were two coming at her, one from each side.

Anna held the saber between her teeth, leaned over the catwalk, and plunged into space, catching a rope that was hanging over a vat of nasty-looking green liquid. A moment later, the two Dwergi on the catwalk made the same leap. To her surprise, they both reached the rope. She reminded herself that they were stronger than they looked: More than one of her countrymen had underestimated these creatures and paid the price.

Anna began to climb, with the two Dwergi in hot pursuit. They were also faster than they looked. Weighing the best way to fight them, she quickly decided on the simplest method.

Taking her sword in hand, she sliced at the rope below her. Her family's steel did not fail her. It cut through easily, and despite all their strength, speed, and evil purpose, the Dwergi fell like stones into the tank of liquid.

The rest of Dracula's servants did not seem to even notice her. They continued to toil, and Anna heard Igor's voice cackle, "We must not lose the master's progeny!"

You will if I have anything to say about it, she thought as she climbed.

Van Helsing waited, clinging to the top of the column with the wooden stake held tightly in his hand, planning to drop onto Dracula. Since Van Helsing was no match for the count in strength or speed, he would need to surprise the monster.

The sound of footsteps told Van Helsing that Dracula was searching for him, stalking through the castle. For all of his fury, the vampire seemed to be going about the task with cold precision.

The count appeared below him. Van Helsing steadied himself and waited for his chance. Then Dracula stepped on the phosphorescent match that Van Helsing had left on the floor.

The match ignited and Dracula looked down. Van Helsing dropped onto him, bringing his weapon to bear. Thrusting down with his arms, he drove the stake straight into the vampire's chest. It was a precise hit, exactly where the count's heart should be.

Van Helsing was on his feet next to Dracula, waiting for the monster to fall. The count stood for a moment . . . and then he smiled. Impossible! No vampire could survive that!

"Hello, Gabriel," Dracula said pleasantly.

Van Helsing froze. The count had addressed him as if he knew him personally and not merely *of* him. As Van Helsing tried to absorb this, he watched Dracula calmly grasp the stake lodged deep in his chest, rip it out, and casually toss it aside.

The gaping wound in the vampire's chest instantly closed up, healing before Van Helsing's stunned eyes. As it did so, the count was looking at him, studying him. "You don't remember, do you?"

"Exactly what should I be remembering?" Van Helsing replied as he backed away into the ancient foyer. Dracula followed in a series of movements that reminded him of a cat who was playing with a trapped mouse.

"You are the great Van Helsing. Trained by monks and mullahs from Tibet to Istanbul. Protected by Rome herself! But like me . . ." The vampire's face darkened before he added: ". . . hunted by all others."

Van Helsing needed time to sort all this out—time he would never have if the creature killed him. "The Knights of the Holy Order know all about *you*, so I guess it's no surprise that you would know about *me.*"

"Oh, but it's much more than that. You and I go back a long way, Gabriel. I know why you have such horrible nightmares. The horrific scenes of ancient battles past? Do you know how you received those triangular scars on your back?"

It was a trick, it had to be, except it *felt* like the truth. "How do you know me?" Van Helsing inquired.

There was a piercing scream from somewhere above: Anna was in trouble. Dracula just smiled. "So, would you like me to refresh your memory? A few details from your sordid past?"

There it was, the thing he wanted most—the end to his search—and Dracula was offering it to him. Van Helsing's response was immediate: He reached into his cloak and pulled out a crucifix. It was forged at the Vatican and blessed by the pope himself. He thrust it at Dracula.

The count shrieked and angrily swatted the cross away; Van Helsing had to struggle to hold on to it. Quickly calming himself, Dracula regained his composure as if nothing had happened. "I guess that's a conversation for another time. But before you go, let me reintroduce myself." He gave a regal, exaggerated bow. "Count Vladislaus Dragulia. Born 1432. *Murdered* 1462."

Van Helsing tightly gripped the cross. It might keep the vampire at bay, but he had no weapon that could actually hurt him. Dracula opened his mouth, his canine teeth lenghtening into razor-sharp fangs. There were more screams, this time from farther away, from the village. Van Helsing recognized the wails of Dracula's brides, and the count spun to look in the direction of Vaseria.

Van Helsing acted quickly, leaping into a large

152

nearby dumbwaiter, a circular blade cutting through one of the cables.

As the dumbwaiter shot up toward the laboratory, Van Helsing saw Dracula spin around to see him make his escape.

Verona flew serenely above the village, looking with pleasure on the carnage, taking joy in the death all around her. "Feed, my lovelies! Feed!"

Running faster, Carl pulled the barmaid along with him. A short distance away, the bride lifted a terrified man, who dangled from her hand, then threw him out over the village. A swarm of smaller bat creatures swooped in like piranha, tearing him to pieces.

All around, the vampire offspring were attacking the villagers and Carl felt a deep fear rising up inside him, not just for his own life but for all of God's world. If this spread, Dracula's spawn could cover the earth. It could be the end of creation.

Nearby, a third-story window burst into shards of glass as a woman hurtled through it. Two of the bat creatures flew out after her and caught her inches before she hit the pavement.

Changing direction, Carl dragged the barmaid around a corner just as the woman was borne up over their heads. The bats were flying low, and before Carl realized what he was doing, he was leaping skyward to try to save the woman. But she was too high up and the vermin carried her off.

There was a scream behind him, and Carl turned

to see the barmaid clinging to a lamppost, nearly upside down and six feet off the ground as a bat creature yanked her farther up by her feet. Grabbing a chair, Carl ran forward and swung it, knocking the monster away. The barmaid dropped into Carl's arms, but his moment of satisfaction was short-lived as the bat recovered and charged them. The girl screamed and Carl heard his own voice joining hers.

But the creature suddenly pulled up two feet short of them, hovering in the air. The look on its face changed from bloodlust to panic. Something was wrong with it. The bat started to claw at its body, and in a terrible instant its very flesh seemed to change, to become molten, and then it burst apart.

Looking up, Carl saw more of the creatures explode one by one, then several at the same time, until they were all gone. Some unfortunate people, who were being carried by the monsters when this occurred, immediately fell to their deaths. The two brides flying nearby gave out piercing shrieks.

Near the top of the rope, Anna was spotted by three of the Dwergi. She started swinging back and forth, seconds later leaping to the catwalk that ringed the inside of the castle tower near the top. She landed hard, drawing her sword.

As soon as she was steady on her feet, she attacked. Her weapon clanged off the nearest Dwerger, bouncing off its face mask. The creature was forced back and nearly off its feet—which, it turned out, weren't nearly as well protected as its face. The princess's saber cut through both legs and the Dwerger fell off the catwalk. Undeterred, the next two charged her together. Anna raced toward them.

She swung at one, hitting it in the chest and forcing it against the wall. She launched a single kick at the other, sending it flying off the catwalk. It gave a short, guttural scream as it fell.

The third one hesitated for just a moment, but it was all Anna needed. She thrust out with her sword, catching the creature in the stomach. The tip of the saber met the stone wall behind it; then she drew it out and the Dwerger fell to the catwalk.

Another kick tossed it over the side.

Racing for the ladder, Anna climbed to the roof. She was pleased to see it empty, but she kept herself alert to any sign of Dracula's servants.

Velkan was lying on a metal table that was connected by wires to the count's terrible machines. It made her furious that Dracula had made her brother, the best of her family, into an instrument of his evil will. She ran to the table, even as a horrific shrieking that could only be from one of Dracula's brides came from the village below.

Velkan looked so dazed that he didn't even see her at first, even as she started unbuckling the belts that restrained him. A sudden clarity filled his delirious eyes. He started shaking his head and pushing her away with his free arm. It was characteristic of Velkan: even now he was trying to protect her.

"Stop, Velkan! Stop it! It's all right. I've come to save *you*," she said. The clock tower behind them began to chime the hour of midnight, and a sudden dread filled her.

Velkan's hand, already bursting with coarse hair, grabbed Anna's mouth. Long claws started to dig into her cheeks. Anna screamed out her pain, her fear for her brother, and the frustration at her own ultimate failure. She had come to save him, as he had done twice for her. But unlike Velkan, Anna had missed. . . .

She pulled against him; Velkan only held her tighter. She would let him cut her face to ribbons before she let Velkan become the instrument of Dracula's will that would destroy the Valerious line. With her anger giving her strength, Anna broke free of her brother's grasp.

Velkan looked at his changing hands and gave his sister a long last look full of pain and regret. As the clock continued to chime, he transformed in front of her, shedding his human skin as the wolf emerged from within. Anna backed away. This time Velkan would not come to save her; this time Velkan was going to—

Someone was behind her. Anna spun around, her hand reaching for her sword.

It was Van Helsing. He had come . . . for her.

"I think we've overstayed our welcome," he said. Calm and utterly confident, with a large, shiny pistol in his hand pointed out toward the very tall trees, he fired a thin tether that flew across the castle moat, straight into the top of a huge oak tree at least two hundred yards away. Van Helsing tied off his end, making the line taut.

The werewolf sat up on the table, breaking the straps that had secured its chest and viciously tearing its way free. Van Helsing went about his business without panic. He scooped Anna up and sprang over the wall in front of them, grabbing the tether with one hand. Anna felt something bang into Van Helsing and was afraid that the beast had gotten him, but the man kept his hold as they started to slide down the line.

There was movement in Anna's peripheral vision. She caught a glimpse of the werewolf slashing at the line. Then she was falling . . .

. . . no, *swinging* . . . out over the moat and into the dark forest. The creature howled behind them as they swooped down to the earth. Anna let go and jumped to the ground, quickly rolling to her feet.

"Are you hurt?" Van Helsing asked.

"No, are you?" she replied. He shook his head.

Anna just looked at him with unbelieving eyes. He had come . . .

For her.

Carl looked out at the village square, astonished. The town was now completely silent. Even the rain had stopped as the survivors surveyed the carnage. Slowly, movement and life returned to the town. People were walking around, looking for loved ones, helping. . . .

"What happened?" the barmaid asked.

"They . . . they just died."

In Carl's second biggest surprise of the day, the barmaid wrapped her arms around him and kissed him on the cheek. "How can I ever repay you?" she asked.

Carl smiled and leaned down to whisper some suggestions into her ear. She looked shocked, but not displeased. "But you can't do that. You're a monk," she said.

"Actually, I'm just a friar. . . ."

"What's the difference?"

"Actually, it's probably easier if I show you."

On the walkway along the parapet of the castle tower, Dracula's brides wept in his arms and would not be comforted. Dracula heard Igor slither up to him; if he had had a tail, it would have been tucked firmly between his legs. He looked terrified. *Wise*, Dracula thought. Still, the mortal had showed some courage simply by coming to face him.

"I am sorry, Master. We try and we try, but I fear we are not so smart as Dr. Frankenstein."

Anger flared in him and the count came astonishingly close to ending his pathetic life, but Dracula knew that Igor was right: As much as it pained him to admit it, Frankenstein had been able to do something that Dracula, in all his greatness, could not. The count merely turned to him and said, "Truly. It is clear that the good doctor took the key to life to his grave."

The werewolf stepped up on the parapet. The creature was all restrained power, its eyes insane by mortal standards. Whatever conflict had existed as Velkan fought the curse was gone. The creature was Dracula's now, the servant of his will.

For all intents and purposes, Velkan Valerious was dead.

In the past, Dracula had told his brides that he was past all feeling, cold, completely hollow inside. But that was not true: he could feel rage. Now his fury was cold, vengeful.

He would have enjoyed killing Van Helsing himself, but he would not leave his brides now. Locking his eyes and will on the werewolf, Dracula said, "Hunt them down. Kill them both."

It snarled viciously and bounded off the parapet.

Rain poured down as Anna and Van Helsing made their way across the moors. Up ahead were ruins that Anna recognized as the remains of the old windmill that had been burned to the ground by the villagers a year before, when Dr. Frankenstein had created his monster.

Death could still strike them at any moment. The creature was out there, hunting them. *No, not the creature: Velkan,* Anna's mind countered. But she knew it wasn't him; her brother was lost to her forever. The thought was like a knife wound in her stomach.

Tonight she had seen him for a few brief moments, only to have him destroyed before her eyes by Dracula's curse. It was too much. Somehow she kept walking, taking step after step when all she wanted to do was fall to the ground and weep for her brother.

But that was an indulgence that she could not afford. *Because I'm the last,* she thought. *The last one standing, the last Valerious.*

As they approached the ruins, she glanced at Van Helsing, who was walking silently beside her, his face a mask. She realized that she could give voice to some of the frustration inside her and raised her voice. *"A wooden stake? A silver crucifix? What do you think, we haven't tried everything before?"*

Then she did something that actually made her feel a bit better: she gave Van Helsing a shove, pushing him under one of the charred windmill sails, which offered them a temporary refuge from the rain even as she continued her tirade. "We've been hunting this creature for more than four hundred years. We've shot him, stabbed him, clubbed him, sprayed him with holy water, and staked him in the heart, and still he lives!"

Van Helsing just looked at her with—what? Interest? A touch of amusement? Whatever it was, it made her angrier, and she brought her face close to his. "Don't you understand?" she seethed. *"Nobody* knows how to kill Dracula!"

With their faces just inches apart, an ironic smile creased Van Helsing's lips. "I could have used that information a little earlier."

Anna just scowled, breathing hard. Van Helsing's

160

dark eyes stared at her. He *liked* being this close to her. *So he is a man after all,* she thought.

"Don't give me that look. I don't need your wolf's eyes undressing me. . . ." She pulled herself away and stared off into the rain. "Not right now, anyway." There it was, out before she realized what she was saying. Anna would not allow herself to hide from the truth.

Van Helsing reached down and picked up an undamaged bottle of absinthe from the ground. Anna looked on, the fight going out of her. She had the feeling she could relax around this man, and he would somehow keep them safe. An illusion, perhaps, but a compelling one nonetheless.

"You were right . . . he isn't my brother anymore," she said, stepping closer to him as he uncorked the bottle. "Do you have any family, Mr. Van Helsing?"

"I'm not sure. I hope to find out someday; that's what keeps me going."

Anna took the bottle and held it up in a toast. "Here's to what keeps you going." A deep slug of the fiery liquid warmed her immediately, and she enjoyed its bite.

"Absinthe. Strong stuff," he remarked.

Anna handed it back. "Don't let it touch your tongue, it'll knock you on your—"

The world shifted under their feet. Anna was pulled downward as the soggy ground beneath them caved in. They fell as a cascade of water and timber crashed down with them.

10

CARL WOKE SLOWLY. IT WAS ODD; THE FRIARY WAS UNUSU-
ally quiet today. His eyes snapped open and he remembered that he was far, far away from the safety
of the friary. He sat up quickly, the events of the last
day racing back to him in a surge of fear.

Glancing about, he saw the barmaid sleeping next
to him, her nude form covered with a blanket. More
memories came rushing back, some of them actually
pleasant, and he smiled. Apparently the day hadn't
been a total horror.

"Ah! Yes . . . no, I remember," he said out loud.

Leaning back against the wall, he felt something
move beneath his shoulder . . . and a secret panel on
the opposite wall of the room swung open. A medieval painting was revealed: a fantastic mural of
two knights facing each other. They were wearing
full body armor and were locked in battle, brandish-
ing shields and swords. White mountains and a large

gothic castle loomed behind them, the castle's largest tower holding a clock.

A full moon hung over the scene, and from one side a white mist crept along as if it were about to engulf the warriors and giving the painting an unearthly look. Latin writing circled the action and Carl began to immediately translate the words, saying them out loud: "Even a man who is pure in heart, and says his prayers by night, may become a wolf when the wolf-bane blooms, and the moon is shining bright . . ." He stepped up closer to finish translating the inscription: ". . . or crave another's blood when the sun goes down, and his body takes to flight."

As soon as he finished, the entire painting came alive in front of him. Trees swayed, grass moved in the wind, and the clock in a distant church tower began to chime. Then, before Carl's amazed eyes, the two knights began to transform: one into a werewolf, the other into a hellish winged beast. The two warriors attacked each other viciously, striking with surprising speed and power.

Carl was shocked and backed away, stumbling, knocking the entire couch over. He landed on the barmaid's semi-nude body. Instantly awake and immediately angry, she shoved him off. When Carl looked up again, he wondered if he had imagined the whole thing.

The barmaid gathered her clothes in a huff. "Friars, monks, priests, you're all the same!" she said.

Of course that was incorrect—there were some

very real differences between each group, and even more between the various orders within each group—but Carl decided that this was not the right time to try to explain that to her.

Van Helsing watched as Anna woke, looking groggy and rubbing her head. She let out a low groan and his hand immediately shot out to cover her mouth. Nodding, he put a finger to his lips.

They had fallen into a very dim, gloomy cavern barely illuminated by tiny crevices in the ceiling. This place must have served as a basement of sorts for the windmill when it had still been in operation, which, from the looks of things above ground and down here, had been some time ago. A fetid stream ran through it, and Van Helsing detected a faint smell of cooked meat.

"Shhhh . . . there's something down here. And it's carnivorous," he whispered, gesturing to a massive pile of rat bones, which had been picked clean. Anna slowly rose, drawing her sword, and Van Helsing started to head downstream.

"Whatever is down here seems to be of human ancestry," he said, pointing out a set of very large boot prints. "I'd say he's a size seventeen. About 360 pounds, eight and a half to nine feet tall. He has a bad gimp in his right leg . . . and three copper teeth."

"How do you know he has copper teeth?" Anna asked.

"Because he's standing right behind you."

The monster stood there, motionless. It was

human in form—more or less—very tall, with extremely pale skin that looked as if it had been sewn together by a child in several places. A rough scar ran across its forehead and, as far as Van Helsing could see, around the rest of its completely bald head. There were other scars that Van Helsing saw on its body through the rags that the creature wore. It looked at least as much animal as man, but it wore an iron brace that ran the length of its entire right leg, which made Van Helsing wonder. Then he caught sight of something else even more baffling: a glowing circular green crystal or piece of glass set in roughly where a human heart would be.

The pretense was gone. Something strange was going on here, but Van Helsing had to put his doubts aside and go to work. He went for his pistols as the monster charged out of the shadows behind Anna and slammed her forward into Van Helsing. Both of them went crashing to the floor, and his revolvers went flying.

The monster was on him in a flash, surprising for something so large and ungainly-looking. Van Helsing felt himself being lifted up over the creature's head and thrown against a stone wall. His shoulder took the brunt of the impact and he fell in a heap on the floor. He could see the creature gazing down at Anna; she met its stare without flinching.

"Oh my God . . . the Frankenstein monster," he said.

"MONSTER?!" the creature boomed. *"Who is the monster here?!"* Van Helsing tried to clear his head as

the thing lifted Anna off the floor. "I have done nothing wrong, and yet you and your kind all wish me dead!" The voice was indignant; the creature sounded remarkably articulate, considering its form.

More mysteries . . . but Van Helsing didn't have time to sort them all out. Business came first. He ran forward and tackled the creature; its head slammed backward into the wall, and incredibly the top half of its head popped off. He grabbed the creature by the neck. Suddenly there was a spark, and he felt a jolt of electrical energy that threw him against the far wall. He landed hard, struggling to stay conscious.

Through blurry vision, he watched it force the top half of his own head back into place. Then he headed for Anna, who backed away until she was standing against some burned timber. "What do you want?" she asked.

"To exist," the creature said mournfully.

As Van Helsing's head cleared, he saw what was wrong with this scene: The monster was not what he appeared to be, at least not entirely. Still there was danger: to him, to the mission, and to Anna. Producing his ivory blowgun from the folds of his cloak, he sent six darts flying, each one hitting the creature's back. Its arms flailed as it tried to swat the darts free.

Van Helsing got up as Anna ran over and picked up one of the revolvers from the ground. "We must kill it," she said, but Van Helsing moved in, grabbing her by the wrist.

"No. Wait."

Frankenstein's creation crashed to his knees, its bleary eyes gazing at them. Amazing: Six darts and it was still conscious. It looked exhausted, beaten, and deeply sad, all at the same time.

"If you value your lives, and the lives of your kind, you *will* kill me," it said.

Van Helsing pushed Anna behind him and approached the miserable creature, whose pathos clearly showed him to be more human than monster and whose breathing was becoming increasingly labored. "If Dracula finds me . . . I am the key to my father's machine . . . the key to *life*, life for Dracula's children."

"He already awakened them, last night," Van Helsing answered.

"Those were just from one bride, from one single birthing, and they died as they did the last time he tried. Only with me can he give them lasting life."

Van Helsing knelt down beside him. "There are more? More of those things?"

The monster's eyes were soulful, lost, and afraid. "Thousands . . . thousands more." Then he passed out, crashing facefirst in the dirt, the sound echoing through the cavern. The gravity of that statement rendered Van Helsing speechless.

Anna lifted the gun and aimed it at Frankenstein's creation. Without thinking, Van Helsing stepped between them.

"You heard what he said," Anna said.

Van Helsing knew she was right. Better to destroy it than to see the whole world perish. It was logical;

in fact, it made perfect sense. But it was something he could not do.

For years, he had wondered what separated him from the monsters he went after. Too often their methods were alike. And he had killed too many times to claim moral purity. But he had never killed an innocent, and he had never allowed an innocent to die without trying to help—even though he had failed more times than he cared to remember.

There may have been a fine line between him and the Mr. Hydes of the world, but Van Helsing realized he was not willing to cross it. "My life, my job . . . is to vanquish evil. I can *sense* evil." It had come from his training, from doing his dark work and from sacrifices he did not want to recall.

Van Helsing continued, "This thing . . . man . . . whatever it is . . . evil may have created it, left its mark on it, but evil does not rule it. So I cannot kill it."

"I can," Anna said, steel in her voice.

"Not while I'm here," Van Helsing said. Their eyes met, transmitting their resolve and purpose. "Your family has spent four hundred years trying to kill Dracula. Maybe this poor creature can help us find a way," he suggested.

Suddenly, Van Helsing caught a scent of something else in the cavern with them. *Wet dog.* He saw a shadow briefly but clearly: the werewolf. Anna saw it as well.

"Oh my God. He's seen us," she said. "Now they'll come for him. And neither you or I will be able to stop them."

Van Helsing grabbed her arm and pulled her along. "I must get him to Rome. We can protect him there." Anna didn't look convinced, and Van Helsing didn't blame her. His plan was in the early stages. In fact, *plan* was a very generous word for what he had in mind.

Frankenstein's creation was much too large to move: If they had to carry him, they wouldn't get two hundred yards. Kneeling down, Van Helsing began to turn him over, and to his surprise, Anna helped him. When he shot her a look, she just shrugged. "We don't have much time," she said.

The "man" was truly a miracle of science and nature. The green crystal bolted into his chest pulsed with unknown energy, and though he looked crudely put together, he was amazingly solid, his muscles firm.

"What now?" Anna asked.

"Somehow we have to get him out of here."

"Look at the size of him! How do you intend to—" Anna began.

"I'm working on it," he snapped back.

Anna shook her head in disgust. "Stay with him. I'll bring a coach," she said, and then, before he could protest, added, "Unless you want to carry him."

In the near-darkness Van Helsing watched the large man lying unconscious, his great chest rising and falling with each breath. A short time later, he heard the approaching coach and climbed out of the cavern to meet it. Anna was driving it and the team of six horses herself.

She brought the horses to a stop and tossed Van

Helsing some heavy rope. "Come on, we don't have much time," she exhorted him.

They worked quickly and were able to pull Frankenstein's creation out of the cave with the rope. It took some doing to get him into the coach. As they sat him up, Anna produced a string of heavy chains and attached his wrists to the back wall. Van Helsing didn't argue; they didn't need any surprises when he woke up.

"Watch him," Anna said, and got out of the coach to return to the driver's bench and take the reins. Van Helsing took a seat opposite their guest and leaned back against the padded wall. The sun was finally coming up. Dracula and his brides could still reach them in daylight, but just the same, he was glad to see the dark of night recede. He allowed himself to close his eyes.

Frankenstein woke slowly. The stranger had done something to him but had not killed him, though Frankenstein had sensed that he could have. It was a mystery, but his surprise at waking at all pushed it aside. It was not the first time he had awoken shocked to be alive. It had happened after the explosion at the windmill when . . .

. . . *he opened one eye, though the eye could show him nothing. Darkness was all around him and pain where the flames and heat had touched him, pain where heavy things were pressing on him.*

A deeper blackness called to him, just as it had when

Father was creating him, though this time the calling was even stronger. It would be easier to let it take him, to return him to the dream he had been having when Father summoned him to life.

It would be easy, but then there would be no one to care for Father.

But Father is gone . . . , a voice in his mind said.

Yes, he remembered now: Father had not survived his last encounter with the Other Man. How long ago was that? An hour? A week? How long had he been fighting darkness? Father was lost to him forever, though his body was right next to him, partly shielding him from the weight that sat above them.

Father had given him life and even after his own death was protecting that life. He would not let those efforts be in vain. He fought the darkness and tried to move his limbs. There was great weight on him everywhere: large wooden beams and some sort of machine. They were very heavy and should have crushed the life out of him.

But Father had made him strong.

He was able to move one hand and push against a beam that lay across them both. It required much from him, but it finally moved.

Holding it up with one hand, he was able to move Father's body with the other, then press up with both hands. He roared with the effort and felt the weight above him stir and shift. His back pressed deeper into the ground, which was soft and wet. Wet. The moisture was important. He struggled to think.

That's what the pain in his throat was: thirst. He needed to drink soon. He pushed harder. The weight above him did not move, but he found himself sinking farther into the ground.

Suddenly the floor beneath him opened up and swallowed him. He fell again. For a moment he was afraid that his life would end when he hit the bottom of some great pit. But he landed not on hard earth but in water. He was underwater and fought his way up.

He found that he could stand on the ground and keep his head and chest above the water. It was dark, but the sounds of pain and fear in his throat came back to him and told him that this place was not very large. He would find a way out. First he leaned down and drank from the pool around him. Then the pain in his throat lessened, leaving a dozen other aches in his body.

Reaching behind him, he found Father's body. Then he began to explore the area around him and quickly located a wall made of stone. He pulled himself and Father out of the water. He felt about in the dark and found stairs. He realized he was in an underground part of the windmill.

He carried Father up the stairs and found a hatch at the top. He tested it with one hand and found that it would not budge. Placing Father gently on the stairs, he pushed with both hands and felt it open—part of the wreckage of the windmill had landed on top of the hatch.

The hatch burst open, pushing aside whatever had fallen on it. Putting his head through, he saw that the charred remains of the windmill were all around him. But the blackened beams were cool, which told him that at least one day had passed, perhaps more. In fact, he was sure that even more time had passed, though it was impossible to tell how much.

He smelled the air. It smelled burned, like death. Moving as quickly as he could, he leaned down and picked up Father. In the cool night air, he could gradually distinguish between the different sources of discomfort from among the mass of pain that tormented his body. His skin felt as though it were on fire in a number of places. And there were piercing sensations in his chest and one of his legs. It was bad, but he knew he would live.

This gave him some satisfaction. Father's dream for him would not die. He knew he would have to be careful. The angry people might be anywhere. Suddenly he was glad that it was night and he could move around unseen. He would have to find someplace to hide in the daytime.

A new pain—this one in his stomach—announced itself. He would have to find food as well. That would have to wait, however. There was something he had to do first. Looking up, he saw Father's castle and started walking toward it.

A few minutes later, he reached a small patch of trees near the castle wall. It was a good spot. The trees would protect him from prying eyes if any of the angry people were out in the night.

Placing Father on the ground, he began to dig with his hands. He did this for several minutes before he gave any thought to what he was doing—he must bury Father. Perhaps Igor was right: perhaps he was a monster. But Father was a man . . . a great man . . . and they were buried when they died.

He did not know how he knew that, but he was certain of it. Tossing the earth out of the growing hole with his hands, ignoring the protests of pain from his injured body.

When the hole was almost his own height, he judged it deep enough. Then he picked up Father and, as gently as he could, set him down inside.

In the distance, light began to show in the sky. He did not have long. He climbed out of the hole. Working quickly, he covered Father with the earth, pushing it with both hands. When it was even with the surrounding ground, he covered the grave with leaves.

"Good-bye," he said, looking down, his cheeks moist once again. "You will be safe now, Father." Perhaps Father had returned to the dream from which he himself had awoken in Father's castle. But even now the memory of that dream was fading from his mind.

More tears, for now he was truly alone. And he had questions that only Father could answer. Why had he been created? What was his purpose? Was he a monster . . . or a man?

How was it that he had not even existed before Father had summoned him to life, and yet, he knew things? He had language, and he knew that the dawn would come soon, though he had never seen it.

Questions and no answers . . .

He looked up, as if he expected to find the answers written in the sky. Instead he saw the castle looming above him. Then with certainty, he knew that the answers might be in there. And Father might yet speak to him. . . .

11

"WHY DIDN'T YOU KILL ME?" THE GIANT'S VOICE BROKE through approaching sleep.

Van Helsing's eyes snapped open, instantly alert. "I'm not a murderer."

"Why don't you leave me alone, then?"

"Dracula's servant, the werewolf, saw you in the cavern. It was no longer safe. I'm taking you to Rome. We can protect you there."

"This is not a good idea."

"It's the best I can do under the circumstances. By the way, I am Gabriel Van Helsing."

The giant man nodded back and said, "You can call me by my father's name: Frankenstein."

"My companion is Anna Valerious." Van Helsing gestured to the front of the coach.

"This is a very bad idea. You are a dangerous man, Gabriel Van Helsing. A very dangerous man," Frankenstein said.

Van Helsing nodded. "I get that a lot," he said.

Frankenstein rattled the confining chains. "You don't trust me."

"It's not personal; I don't trust *anyone*," Van Helsing said. There was a moment of silence between them, but Van Helsing had questions that couldn't wait. "You talked about your *father*, but you were . . . created."

"By Dr. Victor Frankenstein. I was assembled from the bodies of seven different men. My father discovered the secret of life and after he gave me form, he gave me life," Frankenstein explained. "He did this under the influence of Count Dracula. On the night of my awakening, my Father realized Dracula's ultimate plan. He refused to help and the count murdered him. That same night, the villagers stormed the castle. They thought me a monster and tried to kill me. They believe me dead, and for the last year I have been able to live in peace."

"If this all happened on the night you were created, how do you know about Dracula and how you were created? And you speak? How?" Van Helsing asked.

"The parts that Father used to create me had lived before. I have no memory of any previous life, but I have speech, I can read. And while my father was creating me, we were . . . connected somehow. I heard him in a way. After he died, I returned to his lab and read his journals and notes, which I later destroyed so that Dracula could not use them for his plans. Father was under Dracula's influence for a long time, but I believe he was a brilliant man, a good man—driven nearly mad in the end, but a good man. And when he broke free of Dracula's grip, he was strong," Frankenstein concluded, a tinge of pride in his voice.

Van Helsing was touched by the reverence in Frankenstein's voice when he talked about his creator. Despite his odd form, there was a quiet dignity in him. It was truly remarkable: He had lived before but retained no memory of his previous life. Humans wanted him dead. Dracula wanted him for something worse . . . and yet, all he wanted for himself was to live.

A few minutes later they approached Valerious Manor, and Van Helsing could see Carl waiting outside for him. The friar seemed anxious, so Van Helsing jumped out of the coach even before it had fully stopped and asked, "What is it?"

Carl stood fixed for a moment, staring past him, at Frankenstein. "Who . . . ?"

Van Helsing closed the door behind him and told Carl a very quick version of the story of Dr. Frankenstein, his creation, and their connection to Dracula.

Satisfied, Carl finally informed Van Helsing of his own experience with the painting that had come to life. Van Helsing had no trouble believing it. After all, he had seen stranger things on this assignment, especially in the last hour.

"What does it mean?" was Van Helsing's only question.

"I don't know."

Anna joined them and opened the door to the

coach, revealing Frankenstein once more. Carl gaped at the giant again. Van Helsing nudged the friar. "Whatever you do, don't stare at him."

"I'm staring at him . . . ," Carl responded, almost trancelike. Then he quickly turned away. "Is that a man?"

Van Helsing roughly shoved Carl up into the coach seat opposite Frankenstein. "Actually, it's seven men—parts of them, anyway."

Immediately, Frankenstein furiously struggled to break the chains that bound him. "By exposing me, you have condemned me! Me and all of humanity!"

Anna slammed the door shut, gesturing to the horses. "Nothing is faster than Transylvanian steeds. Not even a werewolf. Anything else, you're on your own." Then she turned to go. Van Helsing didn't like the idea of letting her out of his sight, but in this case it was unavoidable. She was only following his instructions. . . .

Climbing into the driver's seat, he tugged at the reins and shouted at the horses. They were well trained and raced away.

Van Helsing drove the team of six through the day, from the time the sun rose until it began to set again. Anna had not been exaggerating: The horses were not only fast but they had tremendous stamina, galloping tirelessly until full darkness descended upon them.

Not stopping to rest, Van Helsing drove the team through the dark forest. Turning his head, he caught a glimpse of the unmistakable forms of bat creatures, Dracula's brides, then lost track of them as they darted over the trees. A whole day of riding and the count's consorts had found them so easily. Van Helsing had destroyed one of the brides in the village, but he had no illusions about that encounter: He had been lucky.

Reaching for his crossbow, he prepared himself. There was a rush of movement, and then Van Helsing was lifted right off the driver's seat and into the air, sending his weapon flying.

He fought the claws that gripped him and then felt himself falling, almost instantly landing on one of the horses while fighting to keep his balance. He was on one of the lead horses of the team. He was safe for the moment, but the brides could be anywhere.

Looking ahead, he realized that the situation was moving from bad to worse.

Just ahead, the path they were on made a hairpin turn, and beyond the turn was a long drop. Van Helsing could not see how deep it was in the darkness of the night, but he could tell that it was deep enough.

If he slowed the horses now, they might have a chance of making the turn. But he wasn't on the reins; he was sitting astride one of the steeds. And by the time he got to the driver's seat, it would all be over.

The coach shook violently and Frankenstein bellowed, "Free me! Let me fight! Let me die! But do not let me be taken alive!"

They hit a bump and Frankenstein was thrown forward at Carl, who screamed. At the last instant, the chains stopped the giant's forward motion and he became still.

"Let me go," Frankenstein pleaded.

Carl shook his head. "Where are you going to go?" he asked. "I don't know if you've looked in the mirror lately, but you kind of stick out in a crowd."

Van Helsing jumped from the front horse to the one directly behind it. Another leap took him to the rear horse, and he didn't hesitate for a moment before he made his final jump up to the driver's seat.

One of the vampires struck him, hard, knocking him back onto the rear horse. By now the team was already struggling to negotiate the sharp turn. Van Helsing knew they wouldn't make it. Still, he held on.

He heard the couplings snap and the coach skidded sideways, careening out into the void. *That's it,* Van Helsing thought as he spun down to a sitting position on the horse. The coach spiraled through the air, then plummeted to the valley floor far below.

Verona watched the coach sail over the cliff. *No!* she screamed in her mind. They were so close to realizing the master's plan—so close to the future she had dreamed of for centuries now.

"We must not let him be destroyed!" she shouted.

She dove for the falling coach, sensing Aleera nearby and doing the same. She reached it quickly and grabbed to the roof with her lower claws. A sea," she said at last. Van Helsing looked at her. Her face was wistful.

You may never live long enough to see it, he thought, and found that this saddened him. Even after witnessing so much death in the last seven years of his life—so much life wasted—he was moved by the simple desire of a young girl to view something she had never seen before. He made a mental note to tell her a bit about the ocean when they had a moment.

"I'll bet it's beautiful," Anna mused sadly, and started toward the castle. But Van Helsing grabbed for her, pulling her back.

"There are those who go through the front door," he said, indicating the place where a lightning flash illuminated a dozen corpses tangled in the foliage, "and there are those who get to live just a little bit longer."

Anna's instincts for this work were very good; what she lacked was experience. If she survived, she might eventually get to be as good as he was. Van Helsing found himself hoping that she would retire from this awful business before she . . . *becomes like me,* he thought. *Before she trades too much of herself for battles won.*

If Dracula's curse was lifted from this land, there would be no more monsters for her to fight. Perhaps he could keep her safe until then, for once preserving instead of destroying; maybe that would win him back some of the pieces of himself that he had lost along the way.

Van Helsing guided Anna to the back of the castle, where they found a small door that was more of an moment later, Aleera joined her. Still, the coach fell; they slowed its descent, but it was too heavy to stop.

Still hanging on, Verona carefully made her way to the door. She had to reach Frankenstein's monster. Her wings beat wildly, and she strained under the weight of the coach, but she held firm.

She could see Aleera struggling as well. "Save him! Save the monster!" Aleera cried out before being blown off the coach. It was impossibly heavy now, but Verona made it to the door, even as she tried to bear all of the weight herself. Finally she reached out with one claw and ripped the door off its hinges.

Her strength nearly gone, she leaned down to look inside. The coach was empty! No, wait: there were . . . tubes of some kind wrapped around a dozen silver spikes. *Silver!* Hissing in anger, she threw herself free of the trap as the coach crashed into the ground and the world exploded around her.

I'm hurt, her mind cried out. She tried to fly and to heal herself, but found she could do neither. Something was wrong. Looking down, she saw three of the silver spikes in her chest, one over her heart.

No, it was impossible! That man—Van Helsing!

Verona felt herself changing into her human form, transforming *back* . . . for the last time, she sensed.

Dracula's centuries-long hold on her was slipping. Now she saw him for what he was: a monster. And she was . . . she was . . . just a girl. Verona woke as if from a dream. Something was lifted from her heart—no, not her heart: even deeper than that.

For the first time in hundreds of years, she felt a glimmer of peace. It was nearly over now, she saw, as the earth raced up to claim her. That didn't matter. She was free. . . .

Van Helsing watched the vampires struggle with the coach. Finally, the bride who was fighting to keep it from falling let it go, and the coach plummeted the rest of the way. The explosion was devastating: Carl was onto something with that glycerine. Then he saw the bride who had been close to the explosion falling. It had worked! He had gotten her.

One more to go, he thought.

A minute later an identical coach raced out of the forest with Anna in the driver's seat. Carl leaned out the window. Van Helsing could see that an unhappy Frankenstein was still inside.

"Come on! Come on!"

Van Helsing drove his horses forward to keep pace with the second coach, then launched himself from his horse to its buckboard. He landed next to Anna, who was concentrating on the path ahead, but he nudged her and gave her a smile.

Eight hundred pounds of enraged fur jumped over the entire team of six horses in a single bound. Instinct taking over, Van Helsing flung himself off the coach one way as Anna did the same in the other direction. Now Van Helsing was clinging to the side of the coach as the werewolf slammed into the buckboard. Then the creature skidded sideways across the roof, shattering all four of the lanterns mounted on the corners.

The werewolf vanished into the darkness as suddenly as it had appeared as the roof of the coach burst into flames fed by the kerosene from the smashed lanterns.

"Carl!" Anna shouted. Looking around frantically, he saw Anna's face plastered to the window. She was outside, hanging on. From the look on her face, she didn't have long.

Bounding over to the door, he opened it.

With the flames licking at his hands, Van Helsing felt a jolt from the road, lost his tenuous hold on the side of the coach, and fell. Frantically he grabbed for anything he could hold and caught the step at the bottom of the coach with one hand. Now his body was being dragged on the ground at top speed.

His other hand found the front axle just as he lost his grip on the step. Van Helsing clung with one hand to the axle, the rear wheel spinning wildly between his parted legs. He couldn't hold on for much longer, but if he let go he was finished.

"Carl!" he cried out.

Carl heard Van Helsing as he desperately held on to Anna, who was still clinging to the outside of the coach. And something else was wrong: It was getting warmer.

"I can help," Frankenstein offered.

"You won't kill me?" Carl asked.

"Only if you don't hurry."

Van Helsing grimaced in pain. He was barely keeping all five fingers on the axle. Then it was four . . .

. . . three . . .

. . . two . . .

. . . then one. He relinquished his grip and saw the rear wheel racing at him. Before he had time to even close his eyes, something grabbed him from behind. As he was hauled up from his death, he saw Frankenstein leaning out of the coach. Stunned, Van Helsing could do nothing but stare into the large man's face as he was lifted upward and tossed onto the buckboard. A moment later, Anna swung up next to him.

Carl looked at the monster—at Frankenstein—and smiled in relief . . . until he spied something large moving across the rear window and screamed.

The coach roof split open. Fire and smoke poured in as someone else's scream brought him to his senses. Frankenstein looked panic-stricken, crying in terror as the flames licked closer.

Van Helsing saw the inferno devouring the coach, and the werewolf rising up through the fire as if it were emerging from hell itself.

The side door swung open, and Frankenstein and Carl peered out over the edge of the sheer drop only a few feet away.

"Don't look down," Frankenstein warned.

"I'm looking down! I'm looking down!" Carl cried.

The coach roared past the precipice and reentered the forest. The werewolf hunched down, ready to pounce. "Jump!" Van Helsing yelled to Anna.

The princess leaped off the carriage, with Carl and Frankenstein close behind her. Without pausing, Van Helsing drew his guns, aimed at the coupling of the coach, and fired. The horses broke free, and Van Helsing turned and threw himself off.

He sensed rather than saw the werewolf leaping at him through the flames. Spinning in midair, Van Helsing fired both of his guns just as the beast tackled him. It was like being hit by a train as the two crashed into the bushes behind them.

Anna staggered to her feet. She had expected Van Helsing to jump with her, but he had stayed on the carriage at least a little longer, and a second was all that the werewolf would have needed.

Rounding a large tree, she saw him. No, it wasn't Van Helsing: It was Velkan. . . .

That could only mean one thing. Anna pushed the thought aside and ran to her brother. He was nearly naked and lying on the ground. She could see the bullet holes in his chest . . . the holes made by *silver* bullets.

Velkan turned to face her. *He's alive!* her mind rejoiced, and she saw the recognition in his eyes.

Every trace of the werewolf and of Dracula's curse was gone. There was regret on his face, and he gave her a sorrowful look full of pain and apology. *You have nothing to be sorry for,* she said silently. *You fought; you were always the strong one.*

"Forgive me," he said.

She watched him die, felt him die, his body going still. In a single instant, she also saw and felt his final peace, his ultimate freedom from the grip of darkness . . . and all the other chains of this world. But it was impossible. He couldn't leave her—he couldn't die! He was the strong one. . . .

"Velkan! . . . Velkan! . . . Velkan . . . ," she cried as she threw herself onto his body, cradling him gently and kissing him on the cheek. "I *will* see you again." A silent certainty filled her. She would finish their family's fight. In that moment, she imagined that she felt some of her brother's strength and purpose fill her. It was a fancy, she knew, but something was changing inside her, hardening into stone. She would not fail.

There was movement nearby and she saw Van Helsing stagger forward. Before she even knew what she was doing, Anna sprang to her feet and charged him, pummeling him with her fists. "You killed him! You killed him!"

Her blows were strong, fueled by rage and grief. At first he accepted them, but then Van Helsing grabbed her by the wrists and held her tightly. "Now you know why they call me *murderer.*"

Anna looked into his eyes, expecting to see anger or defiance. Instead there was only the most profound sadness she had ever known. Her own rage left her. She stood close to him in silence, then noticed blood on his shirt. Gently she opened his cloak. His shirt was punctured by bloody fang holes. "Oh my God . . . you've been bitten." Stumbling back, she noticed something she had never before seen in his eyes: fear. That troubled her almost as much as the fact of the bite itself.

It was all too much: Velkan and now Van Helsing. Anna turned away . . .

. . . and saw Aleera's hand move with incredible speed the instant before it was upon her. She was flying through the air, and then she struck something and there was only darkness.

Van Helsing spun around in time to see Aleera yanking Anna up into the trees. He ran for them, but the creature rose too high too quickly. Still he followed, racing out onto the side of the nearby cliff as Aleera carried off Anna over the precipice.

Carl and Frankenstein staggered up beside him. The three of them watched helplessly as the silhouettes of Anna and Aleera flew off toward the lights of a distant city.

Van Helsing had just killed Anna's brother, and now he had lost her . . .

. . . the last of the Valerious.

12

MARCHING THROUGH THE NIGHT, BY THE LIGHT OF MORNING Van Helsing, Carl, and Frankenstein could see that they were getting close to Budapest, a city nestled in a lush valley and split in half by the blue Danube River. Even from a distance, Van Helsing noted that it was as magnificent as it was ancient. Founded at the beginning of Christendom by the Romans, Budapest retained part of each period of its history: the towers and battlements of castles, as well as the spires of churches, interspersed with modern houses and palaces.

Van Helsing also marveled at the giant by his side: Frankenstein. He did have a pronounced limp, owing to his iron leg brace, but he seemed to have inexhaustible energy. A few hours later they entered the city, though *staggered* would have been a better term. Frankenstein's face was covered by a hood, but his size still made him stand out. Van Helsing kept pulling his cloak tight around him, hiding the bite marks on his chest. Suddenly a blast of wind hit them, and Van Helsing drew his gun.

Above and in front of them, Aleera was perched on a nearby roof. Clicking her tongue in disapproval, she said, "So much trouble to my Master, so much trouble."

Frankenstein made for her, and Van Helsing could feel waves of anger emanating from him, but he stopped the giant with his hand as the bride giggled.

"You killed Verona. If the Master were capable of love, he would have loved her very much. As for me"—she smiled coquettishly—"now *I* will have the Master's undivided attention."

Van Helsing realized she wasn't there to fight and he found himself feeling disappointed. "What do you want?"

"The Master commands a trade. The monster for the princess."

As Frankenstein continued to glare at Aleera, Van Helsing said, "Somewhere public. Lots of people." Now Frankenstein was looking at *him*, but Van Helsing kept his gaze on the bride. "A place where your master will be less inclined to show his . . . *other side*."

The bride chewed this over for a moment, and then her eyes lit up like a little girl's. "Tomorrow night is All Hallow's Eve! Here in Budapest there is a wonderful masquerade ball." She leaped for joy to a position higher up on the roof. "I love masquerade balls! Vilkova Palace! Midnight!"

She whooped and leaped again, vanishing behind

the roof, in a blast of wind and snow that told Van Helsing that she had transformed into the flying creature. He holstered his gun and turned to go . . . and felt a sudden stab of pain from the bite wound in his chest.

Carl immediately reached for his cloak. "Are you hurt?" the friar asked, concern in his voice. Van Helsing shoved his hand away, but Frankenstein's maddeningly intelligent eyes narrowed. The giant lunged forward and ripped Van Helsing's cloak open, revealing the blood and the puncture wounds in his shirt.

"He has been bitten by a werewolf!" Frankenstein declared.

Automatically, Van Helsing pulled his cloak tightly closed as Frankenstein's face contorted into a twisted smile. "Now you will become that which you have hunted so passionately."

Maybe so, but there is something I have to do before that happens, Van Helsing thought. He drew the blowgun from his cloak and looked at Frankenstein. "I'm sorry."

"May others be as passionate in their hunting of you," Frankenstein responded, his face a heartbreaking mixture of anger and sadness at this sudden betrayal.

They had to hire a horse and cart to move Frankenstein, throwing a canvas sheet over his body to keep suspicion to a minimum. After purchasing new clothes and a few other things they needed, Van Helsing and Carl drove the cart to the palace, hiding themselves in the royal graveyard. They found a mausoleum big enough for their needs and waited there.

Van Helsing changed into his costume, a vaguely royal suit of clothes with a large hat and a spacious enough cloak to hide his special equipment. Carl was dressed as a jester. They would blend in and the masks that covered their eyes would ensure that they were not immediately recognized as gate-crashers.

Outside the mausoleum, they turned and shut the massive, heavy door tight. Van Helsing brought down the iron bar to make certain the door could not be opened from the inside. For now, at least, Frankenstein would be safe from Dracula.

As they walked through the graveyard, Van Helsing saw the last shadows of day stretching like fingers over the area, knowing well that as night fell, Dracula's strength and reach increased.

"According to the books, you won't turn into a werewolf until the rising of your first full moon, two nights from now, and then you'll still be able to fight Dracula's hold over you until the final stroke of midnight."

"Sounds like I have nothing to worry about," Van Helsing said. For years he had worried that he was becoming like the monsters he hunted. In the cavern under the ruins of the windmill, he saw that there was a difference between him and those creatures. He was not a murderer, despite whatever he had had to do in the course of his work. However, two days from now, that distinction would disappear and he would become that which he had fought for as long as he could remember.

"Oh my God, you should be terrified," Carl observed.

Van Helsing shot him a withering look and Carl said, "Oh . . . well, um, that still gives us forty-eight hours to find a solution," and changed the subject, looking back to the mausoleum and asking, "Are you sure he can't get out of there?"

"Not without some help from the dead," Van Helsing replied.

Frankenstein awoke in darkness, vaguely surprised to still be alive. Van Helsing had drugged him again, presumably to trade him for Anna; yet, here he was, alone . . . at least for the moment.

Trying to adjust his eyes to the darkness, he saw there was very little light seeping in from outside. It was enough to tell him where he was: a mausoleum, among the dead. What was Van Helsing thinking? Did he really intend to make a trade? Or would he try to trick Dracula?

Either way, it was a very dangerous game, particularly for Frankenstein. He had to get out of there. Only, his limbs would not respond. Though his eyes could open and move, he could barely turn his head; his body was still in the paralyzing grip of Van Helsing's darts.

He could not afford to wait helplessly where he was. Dracula was too powerful, and although Van

Helsing had courage, he was still only human. Summoning his massive strength, Frankenstein willed his hands to move. After a few seconds of concentrated effort, he was rewarded by a twitch in each wrist. It wasn't much, but it was a start.

Then he heard a sound: a scraping followed by the creaking of a hinge. One of the tombs was opening.

Frankenstein wasn't alone.

Van Helsing and Carl approached an ornate palace door that was twelve feet tall and plated in gold. *And this is the* back *door,* Van Helsing mused. It opened before them as if by a spell. Van Helsing took a step backward. Then he saw the servants opening the door from the inside.

For a second, Van Helsing was concerned they would ask to see an invitation but they simply smiled pleasantly. One of them said, "Welcome."

Van Helsing nodded, and he and Carl entered. The interior was lavishly decorated, the parquet floors intricately detailed, the walls covered with tapestries and gilded moldings in the shape of crowns. The furniture was antique and Van Helsing recognized several periods of European history. People came and went in the hallway, most donning masks and costumes, although some merely wore dark robes. No doubt they were the very richest of Hungarian and pan-European nobility. The entire scene smacked of unbelievable wealth—and decadence.

Van Helsing and Carl followed the crowd toward two great doors that swung open as they drew near, revealing an impressive grand ballroom full of revelers. At least he and Carl could remain anonymous in this sea of hidden faces.

There was an orchestra playing a musical piece he didn't recognize; it must have been a fairly recent composition from a local composer. There was something odd about the music, a touch of dissonance that buzzed in Van Helsing's head. Perhaps it was the werewolf venom working its way into his system.

Gypsy street performers, jugglers, fire-eaters and tightrope walkers and high-wire acrobats—a very peculiar scene, but then again, Van Helsing had never been to a masquerade ball in Budapest before . . . at least, not that he could remember.

"Well, this is different," Carl said, gawking at their surroundings.

"Dracula must have something up his sleeve," Van Helsing said thoughtfully.

"So, in situations like this, do we have a solid plan? Or do we just improvise?" Carl asked.

"A bit of both, actually."

They stepped up to large banquet tables. They were full of every kind of food Van Helsing could think of, and many dishes he had never seen before. The two inhaled deeply.

"Smells wonderful, doesn't it?" Carl said.

"Not everything."

"What do you smell?"

Van Helsing took another breath. "Everything." It was the werewolf venom. "Warm pretzels, juniper bushes, ladies' perfume, and rotted human flesh."

That's what it was that was bothering him. There were undead about, and close by. Dracula and his bride could not be far.

"You really know how to put a damper on the evening."

Anna felt herself floating. The sensation was not unpleasant. She was at a party, a grand one, at that. She had not been to many of them in her life. There were no monsters, no hunts, no death. There was only . . . dancing. She was gliding across the room, her feet barely touching the floor.

A man was there. He was good to her; he was her . . . master. No, her mind rebelled. No man was her master. She was a Valerious, the *last* Valerious. The dream shimmered around her, threatening to pop and disappear. Part of her didn't want it to, even as another part of her knew she needed to be somewhere else, to do something important.

The man in the dream kissed her and she awoke . . . in the hands of a monster, the one her family had been hunting for centuries. And they were dancing. Few members of the Valerious family had ever been this close to the count, and none of them had lived. Dracula looked to be about thirty, with a face that would be handsome if she didn't know a demon hid behind it. His eyes were dark, cold, and lifeless. An earring and long brown hair tied back behind his head completed his sinister aspect.

Dracula spun her on the dance floor and said, "How does it feel to be a puppet on my string?"

Revulsion filled her. He was close, touching her. She tried to struggle, but her body did not obey her commands. Understanding and defiance welled up inside. "I won't let you trade me, Count."

"I have no intention of trading you. And if I know Van Helsing, which I do, he isn't planning on making a trade, either." He dipped her and leaned in close, their lips almost touching. "Neither of us has ever settled for half."

"You make my skin crawl."

"That's not all I could do with your skin," he replied. Dracula took a position behind her, gently caressing her neck. He moved in and she could feel his breath on her neck. He could bite her at any moment, take her life, make her like him. She wanted to pull away, but part of her wanted him to do it, wanted to feel the power that he felt. It would be as easy as giving in to him, a moment of submission for many lifetimes of power. . . . She shook her head. He was doing something to her. Working his will on her. Suddenly, Aleera pulled Anna away. "My turn," she said.

As they danced, Anna felt the woman's skin, soft and cold. Anna watched Dracula smile at them. At random, he grabbed a passing woman, and bit viciously into her neck. There was so much noise and movement that no one but Anna seemed to notice.

The view from the second-floor balcony was much better. The dance floor was crowded, making it hard to see more than a few yards in any direction, but from here Van Helsing was able to find Anna almost immediately. She was dancing with Dracula's one remaining bride, and the implications of that gave him a chill. What were the count's plans for her? Van Helsing had no illusions that Dracula would ever honor a trade, but he had assumed the count planned merely to kill her. This looked much worse.

"There they are," Carl said.

"Something's not right," Van Helsing replied.

"Yes, they're both trying to lead," Carl observed.

"Not that," Van Helsing said, catching sight of Dracula watching the two women with clear pleasure on his face. Apparently, Dracula knew him from the past, but how well had they known each other? Well enough for Dracula to predict his next move? They would find out soon enough.

Looking below, Van Helsing finally saw what he was looking for. "Carl?" he said.

"Yes?"

"I have a plan." That might have been something of an overstatement, but it was a start.

Aleera's voice in Anna's ear was soothing and pleasant. "It's the little things in life that I love. Like that last look in my victim's eyes just before they die."

Anna tried to pull away, but she was still under Dracula's influence. Nevertheless she tried, the effort of battling his will showing on her face. Her predicament seemed to amuse Aleera, who leaned down and licked her on the cheek. "I won't let the Master take you, Anna."

Aleera's canines grew, becoming terrifying fangs as Anna watched in horror. All at once the blood drained from the bride's beautiful, flushed face. "I want him all to myself," she whispered.

Anna's eyes widened, but she could not break free of either Dracula's will or Aleera's grasp. The bride was ready, it would be only seconds now. . . .

And that was when Dracula cut in, giving Aleera a warm smile. "You look famished, my dear. Go get yourself a bite."

Aleera scowled as the count spun Anna around, over to a mirrored wall. "Don't we make a beautiful couple?" he remarked, gesturing at the looking glass. Anna could see herself, but Dracula cast no reflection. "I'm looking for a new bride, Anna. Someone strong and beautiful."

In the mirror, it looked as though Anna were dancing alone, being dipped, spun, and twirled by an invisible force. "All it takes is one bite from me," he said, pulling her tightly to him, their chests crushed together.

"You have no heartbeat," she said.

"Perhaps it just needs to be rekindled," he answered pleasantly. He leaned in for a kiss, but Anna angrily turned her head away. The air changed around them and Anna sensed that Dracula was tiring of the game they were playing. At any moment she was afraid she would feel his mouth on her.

*   *   *

From the balcony, Van Helsing watched Carl work his way through the crowd. He could feel Dracula getting ready to make his move. Finally, the friar was close enough to see Anna and the count. Even Carl seemed to sense something and moved more quickly.

A nearby fire-eater tilted his head up and away from the others, getting ready to perform his trick, then lifted the torch to his mouth. Carl sidled up and gave him a quick, hard shove. As he fell forward, the fire-eater blew flame across the back of Dracula's cape.

Now it was Van Helsing's turn. Jumping over the railing of the balcony, he landed on a high wire that had been used by one of the performers. He didn't remember any wire training in the last seven years, but his instincts told him that he would be all right. He took a step forward, and then another, until he was practically running across the wire.

Reaching out with his knife, he slashed another stray wire nearby, grabbing it and swinging down into the crowd as tightrope walkers fell all around him.

Furious, Dracula grabbed the fire-eater and tossed him clear across the ballroom. Good: the count was distracted. As Van Helsing swooped among the dancers, he saw Anna rushing toward him. He grabbed her around the waist as he passed by and they swung together up into the air, landing on a balcony on the other side of the ballroom and quickly skidding to a stop.

Van Helsing spared a moment to look down. The crowd was looking up at them, and then in unison the entire party removed their masks. Their eyes went yellow, their skin white, and fangs grew long in their mouths. *Vampires,* he thought as they all hissed at him. *A lot of vampires.*

Dracula smiled up at Van Helsing. "Welcome to my summer palace."

That was when Van Helsing's plan *really* went to hell. . . .

A side door burst open and a group of undead charged in, carrying Frankenstein over their heads. The giant was chained tightly and bellowing furiously. A deformed little man sat astride Frankenstein's chest.

"We have him, Master! We have him!"

Dracula gave an evil laugh of triumph. Gesturing to Van Helsing and Anna, he said to his followers, "Enjoy yourselves!"

The entire crowd rushed forward, shrieking like banshees. Anna was already moving. Turning to a nearby decorative suit of armor, she ripped the arm off, sticking her hand down the sleeve and into its metal glove, which was attached to a steel mace bristling with spikes.

Van Helsing didn't know how much good the weapon would do them, but the princess had a pleased look on her face. He yanked her into the hallway and they started running. "Where are we going?" Anna asked, following him.

Van Helsing pointed to a huge stained-glass window depicting angels, cherubs, and saints. "Through that window!"

"Are you out of your mind? We'll be cut to ribbons!"

"Not if you relax when you're going through it," he replied, taking Anna by the hand and starting to race toward the glass. At the last second, he saw something strange about one of the images: a saint who held his hand up as if to say "Stop!" Van Helsing's instincts screaming, he grabbed Anna and skidded to a halt.

"My mistake: wrong window," he said.

"How do you know?" she asked.

"Just a hunch," he replied, smelling something rank and corrupt nearby. He pulled Anna forward, sensing that the vampires were behind them. Soon he could hear Dracula's laugh echoing through the palace. He made a series of turns, hoping to lose them. On instinct again, he led the princess up a set of stairs and through large double doors, the vampires still hot on their trail. Van Helsing and Anna closed and bolted the doors behind them, praying they would hold for at least a few seconds.

Loud pounding fell on the doors, and the two rushed down the hallway. A moment later, Carl raced around a corner to meet them.

The friar saw Van Helsing and Anna running toward him and held up the lava contraption from the Vatican underground armory. "Now I know what it's for," Carl said, a hint of pleasure in his voice. Then he looked to Van Helsing and asked, "Where are we going?"

Van Helsing and Anna both saw that Carl was standing right in front of another large stained-glass exit, and together they said, "Through that window!"

Carl shrugged and pulled the pin on his device, placing it carefully on the floor. Van Helsing and Anna were already moving. They each grabbed one of Carl's arms on the run and took him through the ancient stained glass. They fell two stories and landed in water. Van Helsing's whole body disappeared beneath the surface. When he came up again, he saw that Carl and Anna were nearby. The smell of the place was almost overpowering: It reeked of mold and decay.

They were in some sort of old, rotting catacomb, a dozen or so feet below ground level and surrounded by tunnels connected by paths and fetid streams.

A sudden explosion of light came from the palace above them. A moment later, gouts of flesh and gore dropped all around them. The stench was terrible—and Van Helsing thought vampires smelled bad when they were all in one piece.

"Carl, you're a genius," Van Helsing remarked.

The friar was looking a little worried about what he had just witnessed. "A genius with access to unstable chemicals."

There was more noise behind them and he realized that both his hearing and sense of smell felt as if they had increased in power many times. He turned to see a longboat with Dracula's assistant yelling commands to a dozen or so of those terrible Dwergi . . . and Frankenstein chained to the mast of the boat.

Without even a glance at his companions, Van Helsing swam after the boat. The man and the Dwergi dropped their oars in the water and began to row. Van Helsing swam faster.

The longboat was moving rapidly out of the tunnel and into a larger river. As they passed, a huge iron gate started to drop down behind them. Van Helsing could see the misshapen human patting Frankenstein on the head and leaning down to talk to him. At that distance, Van Helsing shouldn't have been able to hear the twisted little man speak, but he could discern the words as clearly as if they were whispered into his own ears.

"Say good-bye to your friends . . . ," Dracula's servant said in a soothing voice. Frankenstein bellowed in pain and frustration. Igor continued: ". . . because where we are taking you, only God and the Devil know."

Van Helsing tried to will himself to move faster. It would be close, very close. . . .

And then the gate slammed shut in front of him, cutting him off from the longboat and from Frankenstein. The boat was only a short distance away, but it might as well have been a league. Frankenstein's face was a mask of helplessness and hopelessness—a man forlorn who had been hunted by humanity, only to fall into the hands of something much worse.

"I'll find you! . . . I'll get you back and set you free. I swear to God," Van Helsing called out.

A huge dark shadow swooped past, its talons scraping across the metal grating. Sparks flew in front of him. . . . *Dracula!*

"God hasn't helped you in years, Van Helsing. Why should he start now?"

Van Helsing heard Dracula's remaining bride laugh as he watched the two dark shadows fly away. Anna and Carl ran to his side and he felt the princess's hands on him.

"Come on, we've got to beat them back to Castle Frankenstein," she said.

He whirled around and started moving. "Yes, I've got to save that creature," he said.

From behind him he heard Carl say, "Van Helsing!"

He turned to see the friar still staring out through the gate. "I cabled Rome earlier to apprise them of our situation."

The hairs on the back of his neck automatically went up, and suspicion rose inside him. "And what did they say?"

Carl turned to face him, an act that took some effort. "Even if you do somehow kill Dracula . . . Rome orders you to destroy Frankenstein as well."

His anger rose quickly. *"He isn't evil,"* he breathed.

"Yes, but they said he isn't human, either," Carl replied.

Furious, Van Helsing closed in on Carl. "Do they know him? Have they talked with him? Who are they to judge?"

"They want you to destroy him so he can never be used to harm humanity," Carl said, backing away.

Van Helsing grabbed Carl by the throat and lifted him off his feet, barely resisting the urge to squeeze him. "And what of me? Did you tell them what I am to become? Did they tell you how to kill *me?* The correct angle of the stake as it enters my heart?! The exact measure of silver in each bullet?!"

Van Helsing could hear his own voice deepening. He felt flushed and his hands began to bear down on Carl's throat. Suddenly, Anna was between them, trying to force them apart, but Van Helsing held firm, feeling stronger than ever before.

"No . . . I . . . I left you out," Carl choked out.

Of course. Carl was his friend. Carl would try to help him. Van Helsing's rage ebbed, leaving him feeling ashamed. The friar was on the ground, sucking air, struggling for breath. Van Helsing looked at his hands; they were shaking. Through force of will, he got hold of himself, balling his hands into fists and exhaling deeply. The werewolf venom was giving him more than heightened senses. The rage . . . the madness . . .

Van Helsing looked at Anna. "It's starting," he said, but from Anna's face he could see that she already knew.

13

As he drove the carriage back into the heart of Transylvania, Van Helsing reached the undeniable conclusion: he was *changing*. His senses of smell and hearing were astonishingly sharp, and he found he could even see small animals at great distances. It was a predator's vision.

He had not slept in days now; yet, he felt better than he had in his whole life—or at least in the part of it that he could remember. He felt stronger, more energetic, more *alive*.

It would not be long now. Soon he would turn into a monster. He would fight the coming change with everything he had—with every weapon in his personal arsenal—but the curse would soon take him. Until that happened though, he was still a man; he had free will and he could still choose how to spend his last hours.

He *would* save Frankenstein. One of the final acts in his work would not be one of destruction done in the name of God and His Church: It would be to preserve innocent life. All of his conflicting duties and loyalties melted away, replaced with a simple desire to help. It would make the cardinal furious, but that was just a bonus.

And then there was Dracula . . .

Van Helsing knew that he had to destroy the vampire to keep Frankenstein and Anna safe. Yes, there was the rest of the world to consider, but Van Helsing found his own world growing very small. He wasn't going to fight this time for the Vatican, or humanity: He would fight so that an innocent man might know peace; so that the little girl who still lived inside the courageous princess might see the ocean and know a few moments of happiness at the sight.

Fighting and dying for those things would not bother him a bit.

It was late in the afternoon when they approached Castle Frankenstein. He scanned with his predator's eyes and ears. Nothing. There was a scent of corruption in the wind, but it was very faint as he drove the horses at a hard gallop for the last half mile.

When they arrived at the castle, Anna was out of the coach, her sword drawn, before Van Helsing was even on the ground. Carl followed a moment later and gave them small bottles of holy water and crucifixes. It wasn't much, but then again, they really didn't have a plan to begin with.

"The back door, then?" the princess said, a slight smile on her lips.

Van Helsing nodded. They walked around to the rear of the castle and found the secret door they had used last time. Even with his new and improved senses, Van Helsing could detect no sign of Dracula, his bride . . . or Frankenstein.

They hurried along, Van Helsing and Anna taking the stairs two at a time, with Carl struggling to keep up. A few moments later, all three of them raced into the laboratory together. Van Helsing knew instantly that something was terribly wrong. His nose and ears confirmed his fears even before his eyes registered what they were seeing: the laboratory was empty. The scientific equipment had all been moved, and judging by the mess they had left behind, the count and his servants had been in quite a hurry.

"They must have taken all the equipment to Dracula's lab," Van Helsing said, dread creeping into his heart.

"Then we've lost," Anna said.

The words cut like a knife. Even if Dracula didn't act immediately to fulfill his plan, Van Helsing had very little time left before he . . . changed.

"Dracula cannot bring his children to life until the sun sets. We still have time," Carl said.

The princess didn't make any effort to hide her surprise. *"Time?* The sun sets in two hours, and we've been searching for him for more than four hundred years!"

Carl was undeterred and his expression was

deadly serious when he said, *"I* wasn't around for those four hundred years, now, was I?"

The rays of the sun tried to pry through the clouds hovering over Manor Valerious. They were winning the fight now, but in less than two hours, that battle would be lost. Night would descend—perhaps the longest and darkest night the world had ever known.

"So, what did you learn?" Van Helsing asked Carl as they pounded up the stairs of the tower and entered a bedroom that, to Van Helsing, looked as though it had been organized by a librarian. Relics, artifacts, and books were everywhere, arranged in neat piles.

"That Count Dracula was actually the *son* of Valerious the Elder," Carl said. Then he looked at Anna pointedly and added, "The son of your ancestor."

The princess merely shrugged and replied, "Everybody knows that. What else?"

"Oh, uh, right. Well, it all started in 1462, when Dracula was murdered," Carl said.

"Does it say who murdered him?" Van Helsing asked. Dracula had said that he had known Van Helsing in the past. It was impossible . . . or was it? Had Van Helsing somehow been involved in Dracula's death? Had he witnessed the events? Suddenly, Carl seemed to be very close to providing those answers.

"No, just some vague reference to the Left Hand of God."

The friar opened an elaborately inscribed Latin text. "Anyway, according to this, when Dracula died, he made a covenant with the Devil."

"And was given new life," Van Helsing guessed out loud.

"But the only way to sustain that life was by drinking the blood of others," Anna pointed out.

Carl was annoyed at the interruption. "Are you two going to let *me* tell the story?"

"Sorry," Van Helsing and Anna said in unison.

"Your ancestor, having sired this evil creature, went to Rome to seek forgiveness from God, and that's when the bargain was made," Carl continued. "Valerious the Elder was to kill Dracula in return for the eternal salvation of his entire family, right down the line, all the way to you," he said, looking at Anna.

The princess nodded. "But he couldn't do it. As evil as Dracula was, my ancestor could not kill his own son."

Carl pointed out some engravings on the artifacts nearby. "So he banished Dracula to an icy fortress, sending him through a door from which there was no return."

"And then the Devil gave him wings," Anna said, suddenly understanding.

"Yes."

"All right, so where is this door?" Van Helsing asked, impatient.

The friar shrugged. "I don't know, but when the old knight couldn't kill his own son, he left clues so that future generations might do it for him."

"That must be what my father was looking for in here: clues to the door's location," Anna said.

Van Helsing felt an idea rise up. "The door . . . the door . . . of course!"

He rushed out of the room. Racing down the stairs, he flew into the armory to the large map of Transylvania on the wall. Carl and Anna were beside him seconds later. "You said your father spent hours staring at this painting, trying to find Dracula's lair. I think you were right, quite literally."

Van Helsing checked where the frame met the wall. There was no gap: It was seamlessly molded into the wall. Undeterred, he said, "I think this is the door. He just didn't know how to open it."

Carl pointed to the painting. "Look! A Latin inscription. Maybe it works like that painting in the tower." He started mumbling the inscription.

Anna stepped up to Van Helsing. "If this was a door, my father would have opened it long ago," she declared.

To continue reading, Carl shoved a chair aside and saw that a piece of the painting was missing. "I can't finish the inscription. There's a piece missing."

Now it all made sense. Van Helsing pulled out the torn piece of painted cloth that the cardinal had given him. "Your father didn't have this."

"Where did you get that?" Anna asked.

He handed it to Carl. "Finish it."

The friar placed it inside the missing piece of the map: a perfect match. He finished the inscription: " 'Deum lacessat ac inaum imbeat aperiri.' "

211

Van Helsing remembered the cardinal's translation and repeated it. " 'In the name of God, open this door.' "

The painting began to change, starting at the edges and spreading inward. A thick crystal frost washed over the entire image, devouring it until the map disappeared completely. Then the icy exterior began to shimmer and transform until, a few seconds later, they were staring at a large, ancient mirror that had somehow replaced the map.

"A mirror?" Carl wondered out loud.

Anna studied it and finally spoke: "Dracula has no reflection in a mirror."

"Why?" asked Van Helsing.

"Maybe . . . maybe to Dracula, it's not a mirror at all," Anna replied.

On impulse, Van Helsing reached out to touch the looking glass, his hand going straight through and vanishing inside. Suddenly his hand went cold, and Van Helsing inhaled sharply. Carl jumped, and together he and Anna said, *"What? What?"*

"It's cold," Van Helsing said, pulling his hand out and showing the others the snowflakes on his palm. "And it's snowing." Grabbing a torch out of a nearby wall sconce, he said, "See you on the other side."

"Don't worry, we're behind you . . . not *right* behind you, but behind you," Carl sputtered.

Anna grabbed Van Helsing's arm, and for a moment he thought she would try to stop him, but she just said, "Be careful," then let him go.

Van Helsing gave her a nod and stepped into the mirror. . . .

It was cold and snowing steadily on the other side. He had come out of what looked like another ancient mirror encased in a large black obelisk. Anna stepped through a minute later and stood next to him. Together they looked up at a huge medieval fortress that seemed to have been carved straight out of the black rock that made up the icy mountainous landscape around them.

They don't make them like they used to, Van Helsing thought, but then, they had *never* made them like this. The scale of this castle was enormous, with spires and battlements that dwarfed anything Van Helsing had ever seen.

The foundations of the fortress appeared to be rooted in living mountain, the castle's three main towers sprouting from the black rock as if the entire structure had been formed from the stone rather than built. Two bridges that connected the towers high up were the only clear signs that this monstrosity was the work of man and not spewed up by the dark forces of nature.

The edifice was both impressive and forbidding, radiating ominous power. "Castle Dracula," Anna announced.

Carl was nowhere in sight, but there was no time to wait. Van Helsing started toward the castle. He heard noise behind them and turned to see the friar emerge from the mirror. Carl looked up at the fortress, which had clearly been designed to strike fear in anyone who beheld it. It produced the desired effect, judging from the friar's reaction: he spun around and ran straight back into the mirror.

Carl struck it face-first and bounced off, landing on his behind. Well, that settled it: The mirror was a one-way ticket. That suited Van Helsing, as he did not have to escape to complete this mission.

"Wait up," Carl said, running back toward him and Anna.

He gave the princess a look and they proceeded to the castle's door. They would meet this battle head-on. The massive entrance was made of iron, rusted shut, and covered in slippery ice for good measure. The transom above the door was thirty feet up, well out of reach.

"Do we have a plan? It doesn't have to be Wellington's at Waterloo, but some sort of plan would be nice," Carl said.

"We're going to go in there and stop Dracula," Van Helsing replied.

"And kill anything that gets in our way," Anna added.

Carl backed away. "Let me know how that goes—"

There's no time for this, Van Helsing thought, grabbing Carl and Anna by their collars. Before he had time to think about what he was doing, he simply ran up the side of the door. It was vertical and covered with slippery ice. It should have been impossible . . .

But Van Helsing did it anyway. In those few seconds, he relished the sheer power of the werewolf's

214

curse. He carried the princess and the friar right over the transom at the top of the door, then down the other side, controlling their descent so they landed softly on the floor.

Anna and Carl appeared to be in shock. He knew how they felt. "Well, as grateful as I am to be out of the cold, *that* doesn't seem like a good thing," Carl said.

Then it started: the pain, sudden and excruciating. Van Helsing bent over as if he were being stretched and twisted from the inside out.

"Are you feeling okay?" Anna asked him.

An odd sensation came over his face, clouding his vision. Then the fit passed and he was himself again . . . or as close to it as he would ever likely be again. But he couldn't think about the future now—he had a mission, and one last chance to redeem whatever was left of his soul.

They were in a massive foyer with high walls, pillars, and ceilings. Judging from the size of the place, it had not been designed for a man bound by gravity. Covering much of the surface of the interior walls were the cocoons of Dracula's young—thousands of them, with electric wires sticking into each one.

"Oh my God, if he brings all these to life . . . ," Anna began.

". . . the world would be a smorgasbord," Carl finished.

Noise. Someone was coming. Van Helsing saw Dracula's servant, who Anna had told him was named Igor, appear around a corner carrying a large

215

bundle of wires and electrodes. The twisted little man skidded to a stop and looked stunned when he saw them.

"How . . . ? How did you . . . ? It's impossible!" he gasped, then quickly regained his composure, dropped everything in his arms, and ran like hell. Van Helsing quickly produced one of his circular saw blades and threw it. The weapon whistled through the air and caught Igor by his sleeve, pinning him to a rock wall.

"Please! Please don't kill me!" Igor begged as Van Helsing approached him.

"Why?"

"Well, um, I . . . ," Igor said meekly, apparently unable to think of a good reason.

Neither could Van Helsing. He tore the blade out of the wall and raised it to end the evil creature's life when he heard a familiar sound: Frankenstein was bellowing somewhere nearby. The shouting was coming from right next to Igor, through a window with metal bars. There was movement beyond the barrier: a pulley with chains. Van Helsing stuck a torch through the bars and looked down a shaft cut through the stone of the castle.

Far below, Van Helsing saw what could only be a dungeon cell. Inside it and encased in a massive block of ice was Frankenstein, with only the large man's head and neck free. The chains ran through the ice. It was a particularly cruel form of captivity, and Van Helsing could see that Frankenstein was suffering greatly in his frozen prison.

A command rang out from above. "Bring me the monster," Dracula's voice echoed. Looking up, Van Helsing saw that the shaft ran perhaps three hundred feet up.

"My master has awakened," Igor said, a smile on his lips.

The pulley started to rise and the chains snapped taut. Within moments, Frankenstein and the block of ice were lifted from the cell floor.

Fury overtook Van Helsing. He dropped his torch and began to pull furiously at the thick iron bars. They started to twist but Van Helsing couldn't break them, even with his werewolf-venom-fueled strength. The bars actually started to move slightly, and Anna added to his effort, but it was hopeless.

Frankenstein continued to rise and Van Helsing collapsed against the bars, defeated, as the power of his rage seeped away. On his way up the shaft, Frankenstein came eye to eye with Van Helsing, who saw the pain and fear in the large man's eyes—and something else, too: a sense of recognition for Van Helsing's struggle . . . and sympathy.

To his surprise, Frankenstein spoke: "There is a cure."

Van Helsing was too shocked to answer at first. "What?" he finally sputtered.

"Dracula. He has the cure to remove the curse of the werewolf," Frankenstein said.

Then the giant was gone, borne upward to meet his destiny. Desperate, Van Helsing stuck his hand through the bars and for one moment touched the block of ice. He caught a last look at Frankenstein.

"Go! Find the cure! Save *yourself!*" Frankenstein called out to him.

There it was: Frankenstein was a man, not a monster. . . . *I was right to come to save him,* Van Helsing told himself.

He felt Anna's hands on him, pulling him back. "Come on! You heard him! Let's find it."

Van Helsing shook her off. Something was wrong here. "There's one question we haven't asked."

"What's that?" Anna asked.

"Why does Dracula have a cure?"

"I don't care."

"*I* do," Van Helsing replied. He turned to Igor, whose mouth was clamped tight. "Why would he need one?" he asked the twisted creature. Clearly, Igor feared his master's wrath more than he feared Van Helsing.

Carl spoke before Van Helsing could act: "Because the only thing that can kill him . . . is a werewolf. . . ."

"The painting—that's what it meant," Van Helsing said.

Of course: the battle between the two great knights, who became a vampire and a werewolf. That was the final clue—the last missing piece to their puzzle.

"But Dracula has used werewolves to do his bidding for centuries," Anna said.

"Yes, but if one ever had the will to turn on him, he'd need a cure to remove the curse and make it human before it bit him," Carl replied.

Suddenly Van Helsing had a plan and saw his future clearly. Dracula *could* be defeated—he alone was the key to the vampire's destruction. Yet even if he somehow survived the now-inevitable battle with Dracula, there was still the werewolf's curse to fear. This would most likely be the assignment that Van Helsing would not be returning from . . . but perhaps the sacrifice would be worth it if it meant vanquishing mankind's greatest enemy.

Ultimately, it seemed that his fate now rested in the hands of his extraordinary companions.

To Igor he said, "You're going to take these two and lead them to it."

"No I'm not."

Van Helsing stuck the blade under Igor's chin, which changed the wretched creature's mind in a hurry. Igor smiled and said, "Yes I am."

Anna grabbed Van Helsing. "Are you insane?" she questioned.

He shook his head. "Not quite yet."

Carl grabbed Anna and said, "He's right: When the bell begins to toll at midnight, he'll be able to kill Dracula. We just have to find the cure and get it into him before the final stroke."

"Are *you* insane?" Anna asked.

"Actually, I've always sort of wondered," Carl replied.

Van Helsing pulled a small weapon from his cloak. It was a pair of clippers. He held them in front of Igor. "Every time you hesitate, if they even suspect you're misleading them"—turning to Anna, he handed her the weapon—"clip off one of his digits," he told her.

"My pleasure."

"Just make sure to leave him with enough toes to get you there," Van Helsing said.

Looking terrified, Igor pointed to two huge spiral staircases. "The stairs on the right, they lead to the black tower; that's where it is."

"And the stairs on the left?"

Igor hesitated, and Van Helsing reached for the clippers. "The Devil's Tower! Devil's Tower! That's where we reassembled the laboratory. Would I lie to you?"

"Not if you wanted to live." Turning to Carl, Van Helsing said, "If I'm not cured by the twelfth stoke . . ." He took a silver stake from his cloak and handed it to Carl, whose eyes widened.

Carl shook his head. "I don't think I could."

"You must," Van Helsing pressed. It was a burden he didn't want to inflict on Carl, but if the friar didn't do it, the princess would have to. She could and would do it, but Van Helsing didn't want her to have to pay the price for the act.

Carl nodded and took the stake. Grabbing Igor by the scruff of the neck, he pulled the twisted little man toward the stairs. "Come on."

Van Helsing looked into Anna's eyes. Time seemed to stand still. Like him, she was scared and preparing herself for whatever she would have to do. He saw something of himself in her eyes, as well as a number of things that were new, exotic, and exciting—things he wanted to know more about. But most of all he saw something worth fighting for. He had found something more important than the search for his own past.

"Don't get killed," he told her.

She looked up at him, her face filled with conviction for their ultimate goal. "You still don't understand. *It doesn't matter what happens to me*. We must save my family."

Anna started to leave, but he pulled her back. "If you're late, run like hell," he said. She nodded, but he found he couldn't let her go yet. *"Don't be late,"* he said.

She smiled and started to move again, but there was one more thing he had to make clear. Van Helsing pulled her to him and kissed her hard, then softly, then hard again. She returned the same passion. The venom in his veins, Dracula's plan for the world, his own unknown past—all was forgotten, and Van Helsing found himself lost in her. Anna surprised him again by doing something he could never have done: she pulled away. She stared at him, her eyes full of promise, and then turned and ran after Carl.

Dracula watched the Dwergi put the final touches on Victor Frankenstein's equipment. The Frankenstein monster was now not merely bolted but welded into the metal pod and screaming angrily. The count strode over and said, "What are you complaining about?"

As if in response, the entire laboratory sparked to life. Great arcs of electricity shot up and down the walls between the dynamos. The gears kicked in and fan belts snapped taut and began to run.

"This is why you were made: to prove that God is not the only one who can create life!" Dracula cried out in a tone one would use to explain something to a simple-minded child.

Turning a flywheel, the count raised the monster off of the ground. "And now you will give life to my young."

The creature merely yelled in anger and defiance. *Typical of the living: incapable of thinking beyond their own petty existence*, Dracula mused. The monster didn't understand or care that he was part of a new order that would soon spread through the world. And in its ashes, Dracula would create one fashioned by his will, and in his own image.

The count turned the wheel faster.

14

VAN HELSING TOOK THE STAIRS TWO AT A TIME AND THEN three, his heart racing as he felt himself getting closer to the laboratory . . . to Frankenstein . . . to Dracula.

Next to the great spiral staircase was a gash in the rock wall, and he stepped into the breach. He was now about halfway up to the laboratory and perched over a fifteen-story drop. High above him were flashes of light and the sounds of equipment running. He didn't have far to go.

Van Helsing jumped for the chains hanging over the abyss. As he did so, some of the weapons in his cloak fell out. It didn't matter. Nothing in his arsenal would make a difference in the only fight that remained. For Dracula, only one weapon would do, and Van Helsing carried it within him.

He started to climb the chain, picking up speed until his hands were a blur and he raced up the shaft. He found that all fear for himself and worry for the future was melting away. He wanted this battle—craved it.

And soon he would have it.

Igor led Anna and Carl up the stairs of the tower. Clearly the deformed servant of Dracula was conflicted. If he continued to help them, and his master learned of it, he would be killed immediately. If he didn't help them, Anna would start using the clippers. Fortunately, Igor was more concerned with the threat at hand. And after a little prodding, it turned out that he could move pretty fast when he wanted to—and when his life depended on it.

They reached the landing at the top of the stairs, where they saw an arched doorway. Behind it lay salvation for Van Helsing. Though Anna might have failed her brother, she would not fail her family, or even the man who had come for her twice now. Yet, that was not the only reason she wanted to do this, she had to admit. When she had looked into his eyes the last time and when they kissed, she had seen something else: a future.

Up until now her entire life and the lives of her family for generations had been built around righting a wrong of the past. Her father had lived in that past, and he and Velkan had ultimately been consumed by it. Anna herself had never expected to survive.

And now a man without a past of his own had come to show her that another life was possible, a *future* was possible—one that included hope . . . and him.

She stepped into the room. Like everything else in this fortress, it was grotesquely enlarged and looked as if it had been carved out of black stone. In the center of the room was a pedestal, upon which rested a glass jar filled with a clear, jellylike goo. Suspended within was a physician's syringe. Igor was about to enter but Anna held him back.

"I'll go first," she said.

Dracula's servant gave her a nasty look, but the princess ignored him. As she stepped inside, Anna was as alert as she had ever been on a hunt. She noted that all of the windows were barred shut and there was no other entrance. From Dracula's perspective, this made the room easy to defend: there was only one way in and one way out. From hers, it meant there was less of a chance of an unpleasant surprise.

There was the sound of a quick struggle, and Anna turned to receive the nasty surprise she had hoped to avoid. Carl was sent sprawling into the room after being pushed by Igor, while the deformed little man cackled gleefully. "Stay as long as you like!" he invited them.

He pulled a lever on the wall, and a grated metal gate crashed down, locking Anna and Carl inside. Then Igor scurried away, his laughter echoing through the castle.

"Bye-bye!" he shrieked wildly.

Van Helsing was very close. He could hear the equipment accelerating and recognized the sounds from the count's previous attempt to bring his children to life in Castle Frankenstein. This time, however, he was able to identify each minute change and even discern the individual footsteps of the Dwergi amid the noise.

Silently he climbed up out of the shaft and hid behind the now shattered block of ice that had held Frankenstein only moments before. Sparks and fragments of ice rained down on him. He could see great electrical arcs flashing through the new, temporary laboratory. Dwergi scurried about and Dracula lorded over the proceedings. This time the count looked grim and impatient to finish.

In the laboratory ceiling, about twenty feet overhead, was a skylight. Beyond that, on the roof, Van Helsing could see the pod that held Frankenstein suspended in the air by chains. He could hear the giant struggling, railing against his captivity, fighting for the life given to him by his "father," his creator. He was not alone in that battle—not anymore.

Van Helsing started climbing the sheer face of the wall. It should have been impossible for a man, but Van Helsing was less human with each passing minute.

He approached scaffolding that held a Dwerger, who turned as Van Helsing reached him. The creature's goggles were up and Van Helsing got his first look into the eyes of one of the hideous creatures. They had large pupils, dark pits with small rings of white covered by angry red veins.

Before the disgusting thing could scream, Van

Helsing took him with one hand, slammed him into the rock wall, and tossed him into the dark recesses of the laboratory. In the noise and confusion below, no one seemed to notice.

Together, Anna and Carl stared at the syringe sitting inside the jar of vile goo. "Go ahead, grab it," Anna suggested.

"You go ahead and grab it," Carl retorted. "If there's one thing I've learned, it's never be the first one to stick you hand into a viscous material."

Anna was suddenly sure that he was absolutely right. Dracula had made this fortress nearly impenetrable. It only made sense that he would have taken final precautions to ensure that only he could reach the antidote.

There was a familiar reflection in the jar, and Anna spun around to find herself face-to-face with Aleera. "Smart boy," the vampire remarked.

As Carl jumped in fear, Anna moved quickly, jerking him back behind the jar. Aleera dropped to the floor with a smile. "Did I scare you?" she purred.

Clearly terrified, Carl replied, "No."

"Then maybe I need to try a little harder," Aleera said, moving toward them.

Anna drew her sword and swung it against the jar. It fell off its pedestal and crashed to the floor, splattering slime on Aleera. The thick liquid burned like acid into the bride's skin and right through the stone floor.

The vampire howled in pain and rage, sounding

more like the brutal animal she was than the beautiful woman she appeared to be.

Carl was nearly coming unglued by his fear. "See? What did I tell you?!" the friar cried, pointing at what the acid had done.

"Grab it! Grab it! Grab it!" Anna exclaimed, keeping her eye on the stricken Aleera and her sword at the ready. She also kept an eye on Carl as he used the hem of his frock to scoop up the syringe. It burned and smoked against the cloth, and Carl jumped and yelped, but he managed to hold on to it. Seeing that Aleera was not a threat, at least for the moment, Anna took a chance: She grabbed a large piece of glass and scooped up the viscous fluid. Then she ran up to the bars of the gate and flung it at them. As she hoped it would, the acid burned a hole through the iron.

"C'mon!" Anna called to Carl, who raced for the hole, the syringe still searing his frock. When he was close enough, she grabbed him and shoved him outside. "Go! Go! Go!"

Before she could get out herself, a hand that might have been made out of iron took hold and spun her around. Aleera was staring at her again, the burns on her face healing before Anna's eyes. "You can't go until I say you can go."

"Keep running, Carl!" Anna shouted.

"And I'll say you can go when you're dead," Aleera said pleasantly. The bride had healed herself completely now. The last time Anna had been this close to Aleera was in the ballroom of the palace in

Budapest. The princess had been frightened then, but now she felt a calm sense of resolve as the blood of her ancestors ran through her veins.

But while she had determination, Aleera had in-human strength. She grabbed Anna and threw her across the room as a child might toss a doll. The princess skidded over the floor and her sword went flying.

With a flick of his wrists, Van Helsing went sailing into the air and through the open skylight, landing silently on the stone roof. There was a Dwerger on either side of him. One had an iron bar, the other a large wrench.

The creatures were fast, and a few days earlier, they would have given him trouble. Now he simply reached out and caught the iron bar with one hand as he jumped up and kicked the other Dwerger squarely in its stomach. Pulling up on the iron rod, Van Helsing saw that the Dwerger would not let go of it.

Van Helsing flung the bar and the Dwerger into the air. The creature went flying over the waist-high battlement and sailed into space.

Turning around, he faced the remaining Dwerger, which was back on its feet and, remarkably, charging him. It was a last brave act in a life spent serving Dracula's evil will, and it took very little effort for Van Helsing to send it after its companion.

That done, he rushed to Frankenstein's pod as lightning flashed and thunder roared around them.

He was dismayed to see that the three metal strips that secured Frankenstein were welded onto bolts riveted into the center of his chest.

Frankenstein's face registered surprise, gratitude, and . . . happiness at seeing him. Van Helsing nodded.

"This is going to hurt," Van Helsing said.

The large man gritted his teeth. "I am accustomed to pain."

Van Helsing understood that. "Lets you know you're alive."

With his new strength, Van Helsing ripped the first metal strap off easily. Frankenstein grimaced but did not cry out.

Before he could grab the next strap, a bolt of lightning struck the conductor above the pod. As if by a great hand, Van Helsing was tossed into the air. As he sailed away from the pod, he heard Frankenstein roar.

Van Helsing's body hit something hard as he twisted and fell. Clutching wildly, he caught stone with the fingertips of one hand and halted his descent, hanging on for his life. Below him he could see a six-hundred-foot drop down the face of the tower to an icy canyon whose bottom was hidden in shadows.

Just two fingers on the stone battlement . . . just two fingers between life and the abyss. Just a few days before, this fight might have ended right there, but things had changed since then.

Van Helsing pulled himself up, clawing until he had a solid grip on the stone with both hands.

*   *   *

Dracula looked up as the lightning struck the pod and a blast of energy exploded from the device. It flew down the wires and through the equipment, which instantly overloaded, exploding in deafening bursts. Flames and sparks flew everywhere. One of the Dwergi was blown off a dynamo and tossed across the room, its body on fire.

The count called to the storm, *"Give me LIFE!!!"*

He felt the energy surging out of the lab through every door, crack, and stone. It ran down the wires leading to his children and he felt the power, the force—*the life*—surging into them.

Anna staggered to her feet as Aleera strode toward her, the bride's expression maddeningly calm. The princess ran for the nearest wall, grabbing one of the mounted torches. Meeting the wall with one foot, she back-flipped away from it, plunging the torch into Aleera's face. The vampire smiled almost imperceptibly and simply blew it out. With another faint grin, the bride blew out a torch that was still on the wall. Then another. And another. A few moments later, the room was plunged into blackness.

Aleera could see in the dark, which gave her a significant advantage. *As if she doesn't have enough of one already,* Anna thought, stumbling toward the wall. When she reached it, she groped her way around. She needed some room to operate, to maneuver.

Finally she reached the gate that barred the door. If she could only get away . . . A lightning bolt illuminated the landing, and Anna saw Aleera standing just outside, her lips curling in amusement. Before the princess could react, she saw the vampire's fist fly toward her. It was as if she had been hit on the chin with a sledgehammer as she flew across the room. The world went black for a moment, but she fought it, willing herself to remain conscious.

Whatever came next, Anna would face it with eyes open. Groggily she rolled over on the floor. She had to get to her feet. She could feel a wind, and then someone grabbed her from behind. Claws. Aleera had metamorphosed into a bat creature.

She felt herself being lifted into the air. . . .

15

CARL DID THE MATH. THE TRIP DOWN THE GREAT STAIRCASE of one tower, across the ground floor of the castle, then up the stairs of the second tower would take the friar more time than Van Helsing had, even if he didn't run into any obstacles along the way.

God favors the bold, a voice in his mind said—the voice of one of his teachers, one whom he had never particularly liked. Certainly in Carl's life at the Vatican, he had been bold. Some of his interpretations of gospel had been downright revolutionary. And his paper on the real origins of the Church's tenth-century Cluniac reform had caused quite a stir in the friary.

But this wasn't intellectual courage. This was life and death—his. *No, Van Helsing's,* Carl thought. That decided it for him. He muttered a quick prayer asking God for strength and then ran out onto the ancient stone bridge that connected the tower to the one that held Dracula's laboratory.

The bridge was just over six feet across, with only a short railing to prevent him from being swept over the side—a distinct concern, considering the high winds whipping all around. The weather was insane, with lightning flashing and thunder booming and rain pelting him. The wind felt like a malignant force trying to slowly shove him over the edge and into the abyss.

Carl knew it was a mistake to look down, but he could not help it. Turning his head, he looked into the darkness hundreds of feet below. Looking up again, he scanned the ground he had to cover, estimating that the bridge was hundreds of yards across. The real problem was that the way was fraught with huge potholes and piles of rubble.

Just when he thought it couldn't get any worse, a bolt of lightning struck the base of the bridge on the other side. He took one last regretful look back the way he had come—only to see Igor charging at him.

The twisted man was carrying a long metal pole, which he held in front of him as he ran. Carl barely moved out of the way as the pole slammed into the railing next to him. The thing spat sparks and Carl realized it was a cattle prod.

Things had just gotten much worse.

Once his feet were on the ground again, Van Helsing made straight for Frankenstein and the pod . . . and was just a second too late. Another bolt of lightning struck the conductor above the pod and Frankenstein roared again.

Van Helsing heard Dracula below them in the lab call out in triumph, "One more bolt and my young shall live!"

Not if I have anything to do with it, Van Helsing thought.

Then there was momentary silence before Van Helsing heard another sound he recognized: Dracula was transforming into the winged bat creature. *He knows I'm here.*

Well, he had come for a fight. But first he had some other business to finish. He quickly ripped the second and third bands off of Frankenstein's chest. The giant bellowed in pain as the rivets were torn from his breastbone, but he would live.

Van Helsing turned to see the huge bat creature hovering close by: Dracula. He had thought the white creatures the brides became were hideous and formidable, but the count was even larger, much more heavily muscled. Also, the head was far less human, with the face more bat than man. The entire look of the creature was angular, with sharp protruding teeth and red eyes.

Its wingspan was over twenty feet long, with deadly-looking talons on the ends of its arms. As Van Helsing took this in, he had the strange feeling that he was looking at Dracula's true form, one completely devoid of humanity. All there was was malice and bloodlust.

The creature moved swiftly. It swooped down on Van Helsing, throwing him back with its claws. Van Helsing struck Frankenstein's pod and bounced off.

An instant later, he was flying through the air, into the skylight, and down to the lab. It was a sixty-foot drop, and he hit hard.

He was aware of sparks flying, flames billowing, and the incredible fact that he was alive—not merely alive but standing on his feet. In four hundred years Dracula had never faced a foe who had succeeded in doing anything more serious than harassing him.

Tonight, Van Helsing promised himself, all that would change.

Carl immediately backed away several steps from Igor and the cattle prod, but the evil man was quicker than he looked. Lunging forward, Igor swung the prod at the friar's head. Carl barely managed to duck as the weapon struck a pole just above him.

Sparks rained down on Carl's back. Turning toward the other tower, he dashed across the bridge at a dead run with Igor in hot pursuit.

A four-foot hole in the bridge and a leap over a nearby pile of rubble didn't even slow him down.

After his rescuer pulled the last band free, Frankenstein watched as Dracula, in his bat form, knocked Van Helsing down through the skylight. He had to help, but when he stood up, he was still too dazed from the lightning strikes to be of much help.

Before Frankenstein could step away from the pod, he felt a tingle on the back of his neck. By now he recognized the signs and tried to leap away, but his body responded slowly, and before he could

236

move he saw a bright flash. The lightning coursed through him like liquid fire. He screamed in pain as the bolt tossed him into the air and the current surged down into the lab.

That is the third strike that Dracula needs to bring his children to life, Frankenstein thought as he struck the ground and rolled toward the edge of the abyss. Though he was strong, his size worked against him, propelling him toward the fathomless darkness. Clawing at the stone floor, he saw he was close, closer . . . and then was over the side.

Flinging out his hands, he was able to grab onto the edge of the wall. Electrical wire spit out sparks all around him. Still he held on. He would not let Father's dream of life for him die. And he owed something to Van Helsing.

One of the wires touched him, sending its power surging into his body. Involuntarily he released his hold on the edge and started to fall. It was several hundred feet straight down. Father had made him very strong, but there were limits; he would not survive.

Reaching out again, his hand found a wire and clutched it firmly. The wire came loose from the wall, then went taut in his hand. Frankenstein was swinging on a cable, arcing across the outside of the castle like a giant pendulum.

Carl kept running, bobbing and weaving as much as the narrow bridge would allow, with Igor dogging him the entire time. Occasionally he would glance to the side to see the cattle prod strike the ground or railing close by—*very close by* on more than one occasion.

Suddenly the friar saw someone swooping out of the sky, heading straight for him. His first thought was that it was Dracula, but then he realized who it actually was. Carl dove to the ground just in time for the giant to swing over him. Igor, however, was not so lucky. The steel cable Frankenstein clutched caught him across the chest and hurled him over the railing.

As Igor fell screaming into the chasm, the cable caught on a pilaster that jutted out from the bridge's railing. Suddenly, Frankenstein was whipped into the side of the bridge and disappeared below it.

Racing to the railing, Carl looked down to see Frankenstein still miraculously hanging by the wire, dangling just below him, hundreds of feet above nothingness. The large man was slowly losing his grip. He slid down the last five feet of the wire . . . then four . . . then three.

. . . two . . .

. . . one . . .

Frankenstein looked up at Carl and said, "Help . . . me," his voice that of a man forsaken by all others.

"You're supposed to die," Carl said tonelessly.

Frankenstein grimaced, pain on his face—and a deep sadness. "I want to live."

Frankenstein had not been forsaken by *all* others—not by Van Helsing. The man before him had saved Van Helsing's life and wanted nothing more than to live in peace . . . and Carl had nearly disgraced himself before God.

"All right! All right! Hold on! Hold on!"

Carl put the syringe he was carrying between his teeth and grabbed the cable, pulling with all of his might. It was not enough. Frankenstein was just too big, too heavy, and Carl was an academic, not a Van Helsing with werewolf venom running through his veins.

Still, Frankenstein was one of God's creatures—whatever the leaders of the Church might think—and Carl had sworn himself to His service. It was time to appeal to a higher authority than even the cardinal. He said a quick prayer and pulled on the wire. It moved—less than an inch, but it moved.

Another prayer beseeching God to spare this man who had suffered so much already. Carl asked to become the instrument of God's mercy and will. He found new strength, and slowly but surely he found himself able to pull Frankenstein to safety.

The wire suddenly tore loose from the pilaster that held it. The friar went reeling, losing his grip on the wire. He saw Frankenstein swinging away from him, still clutching the line.

Anna could barely move. She couldn't breathe. There were iron bands around her throat. No. Hands.

Opening her eyes, Anna saw Aleera's face in front of her, the one she wore as the bat creature, terrifying and full of hate but retaining enough humanity to look like a perversion.

Aleera smiled. "Be happy in the knowledge that I shall weep over your body."

Anna watched as the creature's fangs grew longer.

Defiance welled up in the princess. She balled her fist, surprised to find that there was still some fight left in her.

Anna willed her hand to strike as Aleera leaned down to bite her. . . .

Something blasted into the room. Anna thought that Van Helsing had used some of Carl's exploding liquid, but she realized what it was—*who* it was. Frankenstein was clutching some sort of rope, bursting through the brick and hitting Aleera squarely in the back.

Anna went sprawling. She rolled to her knees and stood up. She was alive! And for the moment free!

And where there was life, there was hope.

Van Helsing was hurt. Blood was seeping from a few places on his shoulders and back, and there were bruises. More than one rib was probably broken. Still, he felt a rush of energy and power. The werewolf venom was doing its work.

He felt things falling away. His mission. Carl. Anna. He tried to hang on to her but finally he let her fall away as well.

The werewolf's curse would soon be upon him and he knew he must embrace it. Once he started down that path, he knew that he might never return, to himself . . . or to her.

And he didn't have to survive in the end to

complete this mission. He needed to destroy Dracula, to finish the work of Valerious the Elder and remove the count's scourge from the Earth. He *had* to succeed, or all of God's creation on earth would be lost.

The huge winged beast that was Dracula walked through the flames of the laboratory, looking like the Devil himself. Then, before Van Helsing's eyes, the count seemed to shrink. A moment later, Dracula stood before him in his dapper human form.

"You're too late, my friend! My children live!" Dracula declared.

Van Helsing's ears told him the count was speaking the truth. Thousands of them had emerged from their cocoons, ready to be unleashed on the world. They had been created in their father's image, full of hatred for humanity—and they were hungry.

Backing up, Van Helsing tried to buy some more time. "Then the only way to kill them"—he looked out through a window at an ancient-looking clock tower outside—"is to kill you."

A look of inhuman confidence came over Dracula's face, one born of four hundred years of experience defeating every foe who had ever crossed him in the course of his long life. The count had centuries on his side, but Van Helsing had a few new tricks that he was certain Dracula had never seen.

The changes inside him were accelerating.

Aleera lunged for Anna, but Frankenstein pulled the bride back.

Anna moved to help him, but he shook his head. "No! Go help Van Helsing."

In a swift, powerful movement, Frankenstein threw the bride creature across the room; it looked as though he might actually be a match for the undead monster.

Frankenstein looked at Anna. "Now!" he shouted.

She didn't move, only looked into the eyes of the man to whom she now owed her life. "Thank you," she said.

Frankenstein nodded and turned back to Aleera, who by now had recovered, tackling him. Anna scrambled through the smashed window, hearing Carl's voice calling to her.

"Anna! I need some help!"

Fighting to maintain her tenuous hold on the wall of the tower, the princess looked down to see Carl on the stone bridge. The friar was facing a twenty-foot gap in the bridge ahead of him and a six-hundred-foot drop below.

The wind picked up, and it took everything Anna had not to get blown off the wall. "Now is not a good time, Carl!"

16

DRACULA CLOSED IN ON VAN HELSING, WHO LOOKED BACK
at the clock tower and watched as the big minute
hand slammed forward. It was exactly one minute to
midnight. The clock chimed and everything
changed.

"One," he said. Dracula looked confused.

Van Helsing started to shake as raw power seemed
to flood into him from all sides—as well as from inside. A red mist descended over his eyes and he
sensed something within him swelling, at first small
but powerful, then large and overwhelming. Suddenly it seemed as if his skin could no longer contain
him and he felt himself expanding, shedding something unimportant as he grew in power . . . and rage.

He was transforming, and although he tried to
hang on to something of the man he had been and
tried to remember Anna and Carl, he soon found
that he could not even recollect their faces in his
mind's eye.

Only one thing mattered now: Dracula. His Enemy. He felt his muscles throbbing with power and a lust for blood—the blood of the monster before him.

Dracula looked stunned. "No . . . this . . . this is not right," he uttered. Then he was angry. "This cannot be!"

Something else showed in Dracula's eyes: fear. That was good. His Enemy feared him. His Enemy feared the Wolf.

Anna looked at Carl, who was stuck where he was, with no place to go but down into the void. To save Van Helsing, Carl would have to somehow get across the gap with the antidote. Looking around, Anna saw the wire that was hanging nearby, the same one that Frankenstein had used to smash his way into the room. It was crazy, ridiculous, and dangerous—and the only chance they had.

Leaping out from the relative safety of the wall, she grabbed the wire, which hissed and sparked in her hands. Hanging on for dear life, she swung down across the face of the castle as the clock chimed again.

"Two," she remarked as she sailed through space.

His Enemy backed away from him, rightly wary of his power as the Wolf. He felt indestructible; he was running with the moon now.

With a predator's growl, he took a single step forward. For the first time in four hundred years, Dracula took a corresponding step backward in retreat.

244

"You and I are part of the same grand game, Gabriel," the vampire said. *Gabriel . . . Gabriel . . .*, the Wolf thought. The name held meaning for him. Then he remembered: It was his human name. It *had* been his name when a man was all he was. But not anymore. Now he was the Wolf.

His Enemy continued to back away, and the Wolf's predator instinct told him that Dracula was trying to buy time. "But we need not find ourselves on opposite sides of the board . . . ," the vampire cajoled.

The clock chimed three as Anna swung toward the bottom of her arc, just above Carl. The friar stepped to the edge of the bridge and held the syringe in his hand.

"Three!" he called.

Two things happened at once. Anna spotted another cable and released the one she held, while Carl simultaneously threw the syringe. Hurtling through space and grasping the second wire, Anna held out her other hand as the syringe flew toward her.

She didn't miss. Antidote in hand, she began to arc up toward the other tower—toward the laboratory and Van Helsing. She was coming for *him*.

The Wolf lunged at his Enemy, who assumed his winged form and flew up the wall, heading for the open skylight. The Wolf recognized prey that was running in fear and bounded after it, using his claws to climb the sheer wall.

Before the bat creature could reach the opening

and escape into the night, the Wolf leaped out and grabbed his Enemy, and they fell to the floor below, crashing through the machines that lay there.

Explosions. Fire and sparks everywhere. The Wolf howled in exhilaration.

As the clock tower chimed for the fourth time, Anna knew she was close as she sailed up to the laboratory tower. She had to time her jump just right or she would either sail past the tower and fall to her death, or slam into its side.

She saw a flash of white flitting through the gloom. Aleera. *Not now!* her mind screamed. She held fast to the wire and then watched Aleera slice it from above with a swipe of her claw.

Anna's momentum kept her flying through the air. She twisted her body, trying to reach out with her hands, to grab on to something—anything.

She prayed for help, and to her amazement she hit a ledge on the side of the castle wall. Incredibly she didn't fall. The ledge held and she was still in one piece.

Anna began to pull herself up.

Dracula was in human form again. The vampire was trying to confuse him, but the Wolf kept his focus. He had not only the instincts of the Wolf but its animal cunning . . . and something else left from the man he used to be. He remembered that this was the enemy of the whole world . . . a world which it was his job to protect.

Dracula was *his assignment.*

"You're being used, Gabriel. As was I. But I escaped, and so can you!" the Enemy hissed.

The Wolf had heard enough. He flung himself at the Enemy, who changed again, becoming the winged beast once more and using its sharp hands and feet to tear at the Wolf. As the claws struck him, cutting into his hide, the Wolf howled in pain—pain that brought the world into focus, and fueled his rage.

As he slashed at the bat creature, the Wolf reveled in its shrieks. The Enemy threw itself up into the air and into the rafters, where it became a man again. The Enemy was injured, the Wolf was pleased to see: His arm torn and limp at his side.

If the Enemy could be hurt, he could also be killed.

"I know who you are—who controls you! Join me! Join me and I'll cut the strings that play you! I'll give you your life back!" the Enemy said, and the clock chimed again.

The Wolf paused for a moment, resisting the urge to kill. The Enemy was offering him something that had once been important; the Enemy was offering him his life.

But that was before he started running with the moon, before its power ran through his body. The Wolf wanted only one thing now: to kill its Enemy. That thought pushed all others aside.

Just as Anna pulled herself up onto the ledge, Aleera landed next to her. Springing to her feet, the princess began backing up on the narrow shelf as Aleera closed in. A quick look behind her told Anna that the ledge ended after only a few steps.

This could be a very short and one-sided fight.

The Wolf felt the hunger for victory, the hunger for the blood of his Enemy. He bounded to the wall and climbed it, grabbing Dracula and bringing him down to the floor.

Dracula was struggling desperately, pulling away from him. "Don't you understand? Four hundred years ago we were friends. Partners! Brothers!"

The clock chimed. That was important, the Wolf knew. It meant he did not have much time to finish his Enemy.

Dracula changed into the bat creature again and tried to take flight, but he was too injured. There would be no more waiting. The Wolf was on him, putting his claws around his Enemy's throat.

Very close now. He felt the power of the moon and soon he would have his victory.

And then his strength began to fade.

The Wolf looked over one shoulder out a window to see clouds begin to creep in front of the moon.

Fading . . .

Gone . . .

Van Helsing found himself with his hands wrapped around the bat creature's throat. The Wolf was no more and he was just a man again.

Then his training took over and he assessed the situation. He was a human facing perhaps the most powerful supernatural being ever to walk the earth. Dracula had been hurt in the battle against him—but he was still more than a match for an ordinary man.

Staggering backward, Van Helsing saw the creature Dracula had become look out the window at the roiling clouds that were now obscuring the moon. Then it turned to Van Helsing. A confident glint filled the winged beast's eyes.

"Did I mention that it was *you* who murdered me?" Dracula said.

Anna heard the clock chime again, but there was nowhere for her to go: the castle wall was at her back, the pit was on either side, and the demon was facing her.

Aleera stepped in for the kill and said, "Your blood shall make me even more beautiful. What do you think of that?"

There was a flash of light and something pierced Aleera's chest. It had flown through the air and impaled the vampire: a silver stake!

Carl!

Anna looked over at the bridge. Carl had crawled into the gap in the bridge and was hanging between two girders. The friar was still trying to reach the laboratory, and risking his life to do so. Looking back at Aleera, Anna saw the vampire staring at her in surprise and horror. Already she was starting to change. . . .

The vampire's skin started to bubble and run, rotting even as it turned to slime.

"I think if you're going to kill somebody, kill them; don't stand around talking about it," Anna said.

Aleera gurgled something unintelligible and burst in front of her, lumps of putrefied gore flying in all directions. Anna saw the silver stake flash through the air, propelled by the explosion, and embed itself in a beam less than a foot from Carl's head.

The clock chimed once more. Carl looked up at it and cried, *"How many is that?! How many is that?!"*

Anna was already racing across the ledge and onto the parapet walkway that ringed the tower. "Eight," Anna called out, laying on speed. *Just four left.*

Van Helsing backed away from Dracula, moving through the flaming, sparking equipment as the vampire took human form and slowly closed in on him. The count's right hand was still limp at his side, but his left seemed to be fine.

"All I wanted was life, Gabriel. . . . Now I'll have to take yours," Dracula said.

The count held up his left hand, revealing that his ring finger was missing. It looked as if it had been cut off long ago.

"And I'll take my ring back as well," Dracula said.

Reflexively, Van Helsing felt for the band on his own left hand. There was still so much that he did not understand. Who was he? How had he and Dracula been connected? How was it that he had memories from so long ago?

The clock tower chimed again—no time for answers. Van Helsing felt the wall behind him.

He was trapped.

The vampire's teeth grew into long fangs. "Don't be afraid, Gabriel. Now I will give you back your life, your memory," Dracula said.

Looking around desperately, Van Helsing caught sight of the moon outside.

The clouds were just clearing and Van Helsing felt the power surge within him again. The transformation was much faster than before. He was the Wolf once more. Lunging for the Enemy, he grabbed Dracula with his hands, chomping down on the vampire's throat. His teeth tore through flesh and sinew, finally meeting . . . tasting blood as Dracula cried out in agony.

The Wolf stepped back and watched Dracula start to shrivel before his eyes, shrinking and decaying. The great monster, the Enemy to all, was disappearing before his eyes.

The vampire fought, tried to resist, but there were laws that were greater than even his unearthly power could challenge. He had been strong in life, and even stronger in death, but he had risen from dust, and to dust he would return.

As the count wasted away, his screams echoed through the castle. Soon there was no flesh, only ash, a charred husk, and soon not even that. Finally there was only black soot burned into the floor.

The Enemy was no more.

The clock chimed again.

*   *   *

As Anna ran up the stairs to Dracula's makeshift laboratory, she saw the smaller bats that were Dracula's children flying freely through the air. At first she was afraid they would attack her, but they seemed confused, preoccupied. They had trouble keeping themselves aloft.

That's Van Helsing, she hoped.

When they started to explode, she was sure. *He's done it!* she rejoiced. *Somehow he's done it!*

She had waited her whole life for this moment. For generations, her family had thought of nothing else. Her father and brother had died for it. She should have been overjoyed, but she realized that she still had something to do—something that pushed all other thoughts aside.

It wasn't over for Van Helsing. He needed her now; he needed her to come for him. Only seconds remained. Bursting through the door, she beheld the werewolf with his back to her. Holding the syringe tightly in one hand, she charged and heard the clock chime one last time. "Twelve," she said aloud.

But the werewolf was aware of Anna before she even entered the room, and spun to meet her. The curse was still upon him and the moon still held him in its grip. He pounced with a flash of fangs and claws.

Anna screamed as the creature threw itself at her, hundreds of pounds of raging fury driving her back through the air. She lunged with the syringe and caught the werewolf directly in the chest.

Something struck her hard from behind, and she realized that they had crashed onto a piece of furniture that had then broken beneath her.

That's not the only thing that's broken, her mind called out.

She tried to get up, to push the beast off of her, but found that none of her limbs would obey her commands.

The werewolf was on top of her, but he wasn't moving. He hadn't gone for the kill. Then she saw the empty syringe sticking out of his chest and realized that nothing was wrong.

She had come for Van Helsing, and she hadn't failed him.

Anna willed her resisting body to move again and realized that she might not be getting up from this fight, but it didn't matter.

They had won: they had rid the world of Dracula's curse. The count's children were dead, as were his brides. The man who had risked so much for them all—for her—would soon be free.

Anna had been a soldier in a war. There was a price to be paid even for victory, and she would gladly pay it.

Looking up, she could see that there was pain and confusion in the werewolf's eyes. Anna wanted to say something, but found that her mouth also would not obey her.

It was all right. A gentle peace descended on her. The world would have a future, Van Helsing would have a future—not with her, but he would have one.

Anna found comfort in her past. Papa. Mama. Velkan. Images swirled in her mind. Memories. Good feelings.

And there was a beautiful dream that had been interrupted, that she felt reclaiming her. Her instinct was to fight, but Anna resisted it this time. Her time for fighting was past. . . .

Anna let herself go and fell into the dream's embrace.

When Carl ran into the room, the werewolf was on top of Anna. He skidded to a stop, not able to tell if she was alive or not, but he was sure of one thing: It was midnight and the werewolf was still here. He was too late: Van Helsing was lost.

Gabriel Van Helsing had vanquished Dracula, saving humanity from the vampire's scourge. Van Helsing was a great man who had fought many battles in the service of God, and he had paid a terrible price for each victory—but none as terrible as this: He had become that which he hunted. He had become an instrument of evil, the one fear that Carl knew he had.

There was nothing the friar could do to save him now, but there was something he could do to free him. Reaching into his robe, Carl pulled out a sliver stake. His hand trembled and he prayed for strength.

"God forgive me."

Running forward, he brought it down with all of his might, aiming for the center of the werewolf's back, for the creature's heart—*no, Van Helsing's heart,* his mind corrected.

Even as the blade plunged toward its mark, he knew that his aim was true. And then, in a movement that was almost too quick to follow, the werewolf spun around. A claw shot out and grabbed Carl's wrist, stopping the stake just short before it penetrated his hide.

Carl felt a knot of fear rise up from his stomach. The beast would strike quickly now. He braced himself, and prepared to give his accounting to God.

The creature twitched but did not strike. Instead, his red eyes stared at the friar, first with a blazing fury and then something else: perhaps recognition. Then the werewolf turned slightly to face him and Carl saw the syringe sticking out of his chest, empty. The werewolf released him and Carl stumbled back.

Reaching for his chest, the creature ripped the syringe out and threw it away. Then he looked down at Anna. Carl did the same. She was still and her eyes were wide open. The friar's fear melted into grief, and then he saw the terrible understanding on the werewolf's face.

"She's dead," Carl said, scarcely believing the words himself. She had fought her entire life against the forces of darkness. In that, she had been Van Helsing's equal. Looking at the werewolf now, the friar realized that, to him, she had meant much more than that.

The werewolf crouched over Anna, who even in

death seemed beautiful, lying on the broken couch. Behind the creature, the arched window showed the full moon in all its glory. The beast tilted his head back and gave a terrible howl, baying mournfully at the moon.

The roar seemed to go on forever. Then it began to change—the creature began to grow smaller. A few moments later Van Helsing was himself again, crying out his very human pain and anguish.

Epilogue

THEY APPROACHED THE BLACK SEA LATE THE NEXT NIGHT. Carl had driven the horses for the entire trip, which allowed Van Helsing to remain inside the coach with Anna. He could not leave her. Soon he would have no choice, but for the few hours of the ride he stayed with her, not even closing his eyes to rest. There would be time enough for that later.

Physically, he felt fine. The werewolf venom had healed his body, though it could do nothing for his spirit.

Anna had fought so long and so hard that Van Helsing had thought she was indestructible. She had faced werewolves and vampires and had survived them all. *All except me,* he thought bitterly.

He smelled the sea before he saw it in moonlight. They were close now, but he realized that he was in no hurry to complete this task. Carl drove the team up through the mountain passes. When Van Helsing saw the spot he was looking for, he called for the friar to stop.

Carl offered to help him, but Van Helsing insisted on building the pyre himself. It was the least he could do for her—*after I killed her*—his mind accused. Of course, he had not been able to control himself; no one would have been able to in the same situation.

Van Helsing understood that perfectly and found that it made not a bit of difference. He should have found a way. It had been his assignment to protect her. The cardinal had wanted her safe until Dracula was destroyed, and Van Helsing had accomplished that much. But Van Helsing knew that he wanted to give her more than temporary protection. He had wanted to give her a life free of her family's struggle.

A life with me, he thought. Yes, it was true, and Van Helsing would not deny it. He was angry for her, for himself, and at the one power who could have prevented this but chose not to—the power that demanded so much sacrifice from the Valerious family and from a beautiful and strong young woman whose only dream was to see the sea.

Van Helsing would not deny her the fulfillment of that dream.

By the time he finished the pyre, the sun was beginning to rise in the sky, its first light playing over the waters of the Black Sea. The view from their mountain perch was beautiful, and Van Helsing knew that Anna would have enjoyed it. *You have to look on the brighter side of death,* she had once told him. It was her way—the Transylvanian way.

But it was not *his* way.

There was nothing but pain and loss here . . . and sacrifice.

Carl performed the funeral rite and read from the Bible, tears streaming down his face. He was a good man and had fought hard in his way. A large part of the victory over Dracula belonged to him, but Van Helsing saw that Carl was paying his own price for it.

That was Van Helsing's fault. He had insisted that the friar leave the safety of the Vatican to come on this mission. Van Helsing had thought Carl would learn a few things about life in the field. Now he wished he could spare his friend the terrible knowledge those lessons brought with them.

It was another burden Van Helsing knew he had to bear. He wondered if the cardinal, who had sent him on so many assignments, also felt the weight of that responsibility. What price had the cardinal paid for Van Helsing's victories? What burden did Jinette bear?

Carl finished the service and closed the Bible slowly, as if reluctant to bring it to an end and finally commend her to the next world. Like Van Helsing's taking her to the sea, the funeral rite was the last thing Carl could do for Anna. Now there was nothing else left.

No, there was one more task that remained to be fulfilled, and this one was Van Helsing's alone. He stepped forward and touched the torch to the pyre. It burned quickly, and soon the flames were warming his face.

*   *   *

Frankenstein watched the burning pyre from his raft as he drifted out to sea. He removed his hat in respect. Van Helsing had been silent the entire trip in the coach, merely staring at Anna. Her loss had been a blow to him, one that Frankenstein had understood.

His life had not been long, but he had known loss. His time with Father had been heartbreakingly short and in the end Father had died fighting against the same darkness that swallowed Anna. And though the princess had died, she had given Van Helsing life, the same gift that Father had given him.

Frankenstein vowed that he would not waste his Father's gift.

Van Helsing had the strangest feeling that he was being watched. He looked around and saw no one but Carl, and Frankenstein in the distance on the Black Sea. There was no one else here, for although Anna's body would be with them for a few more minutes, in every way that mattered she was gone.

As he watched the pyre burn, he saw the smoke swirl and move. Tendrils of smoke wafted out, like long wispy fingers, and lifted his chin up with a force that was irresistible even though it was invisible. For a moment he thought he recognized the touch, the strength.

Anna wasn't gone—not yet. He saw her face in the smoke. Van Helsing had no doubt that she was with him. The face smiled and floated up to the reddening dawn sky.

Stunned, he took a step forward, wanting to follow. Then he saw something that stopped him where he stood. There were other faces with Anna's. Van Helsing recognized Velkan and Anna's father, a woman who must have been her mother . . . and others. The entire Valerious line. Anna's father hugged her; her mother was tending to her hair; Velkan was beaming his love and pride.

Anna's past and future merged into one, and Van Helsing saw that she was happy, *felt* that she was happy. And then he understood her final gift: a feeling of peace that descended on him; peace and hope—for him, for a giant of a man on a small raft in a very large sea, for everyone.

Van Helsing felt a hand on his shoulder. He turned to find that Carl was witnessing the vision, too. Anna gave him one last look, her radiant eyes beaming with happiness, with hope, with all possibility. And finally she and the rest of her family ascended into the dawn sky.

Her fight was over. She had come out on the other side . . . the brighter side.

As the pyre burned to embers, Van Helsing and Carl saddled up two of the horses. Mounting his stallion, Van Helsing patted the strong black horse, feeling its strength. *Transylvanian steeds*, he thought. *Nothing faster.*

With Carl beside him, Van Helsing rode through an endless golden wheat field, which turned red in the spreading light of the morning sun.

About the Author

Kevin Ryan is the author of the bestselling trilogy *Star Trek*®: *Errand of Vengeance* and the co-author (with Michael Jan Friedman) of *Star Trek: The Next Generation*®—*Requiem*. He has also written two books for the Roswell series. In addition, Kevin has published a number of comic books and written for television. He lives in New York with his wife and four children. He can be reached at Kryan1964@aol.com.

WITNESS THE BEGINNING

WITH THE ALL-NEW
ORIGINAL ANIMATED FILM PREQUEL,

VAN HELSING
THE LONDON ASSIGNMENT

- Features the voice of *Van Helsing* star Hugh Jackman (*X-Men, X2: X-Men United*)
- Premiering exclusively on DVD
- Loaded with bonus features, including an in-depth look at *Van Helsing*'s groundbreaking special effects
- From the director and producers of the motion picture *Van Helsing* – Stephen Sommers and Bob Ducsay

OWN THE DVD MAY 11